Charlotte's Choice

Charlotte's Choice

by Cathleen Twomey

Boyds Mills Press

For my parents,
Edward J. and Catherine V. Twomey,
who filled my childhood with books,
music, and unconditional love.

Copyright © 2001 by Cathleen Twomey

Published by Boyds Mills Press, Inc.
A Highlights Company
815 Church Street
Honesdale, Pennsylvania 18431
Printed in the United States of America
Visit our Web site at: www.boydsmillspress.com

U.S. Cataloging-in-Publication Data
(Library of Congress Standards)

Twomey, Cathleen.
  Charlotte's choice / by Cathleen Twomey. — 1st ed.
[184] p. ; cm.
Summary: A young woman, burdened by a terrible secret, must decide to reveal the
secret and betray her best friend or to keep the secret and send her friend to prison in
this coming-of-age story set in Missouri in 1905.
ISBN: 1-56397-938-1
1. Best friends — Fiction — Juvenile literature. 2. Missouri — History —
Juvenile fiction. 3. Values — Fiction — Juvenile literature. [1. Best friends —
Fiction. 2. Missouri — History — Fiction. 3. Values —Fiction.]
I. Title.
  [F] 21   2001   CIP
2001087907

First edition, 2001
Book designed by Pat Linder
Edited by Greg Linder
The text of this book is set in 12.5-point Cochin.

10 9 8 7 6 5 4 3 2 1

Acknowledgments

Many thanks to:
My father, Edward J. Twomey, who listens without judging and offers unquestioning support; Greg Linder, my editor, for his insight and thoughtful guidance; Kent Brown, Jr.; Edward Twomey and Mary Twomey; Peggy Derrivan Purington; Fred Bailey, Carol Frizzell, and my students at Groveton High School; the North Country Writer's Group (Eleanor Mason, Hannah Lenehan, Dave Killam, Steve Bissonnette, Valerie Herres, Bob Every, Judy Todd, Mark Roberts, Bob Christie, and Maryellen Cannon); Susi Richardson, the Bear Writers, and Inklings; the faculty and students of Vermont College's Master of Fine Arts in Writing for Children program, especially Marion Dane Bauer, Jane Resh Thomas, Norma Fox Mazer, and "The Cave"; Nancy Scroggins and the staff of the Northumberland Public Library; and Geneva and the crew at Groveton Market.

Contents

Turner's Crossing

My mother always says it's impossible to grow up right and proud if you have no sense of where you came from or where you're going.

Now, a lot that Ma rattles on about I don't understand, and a lot more I don't agree with. But she's right about place giving you a sense of who you are. All my life, I've been Charlotte Ann Matthews of Turner's Crossing, Missouri. For better or worse, that about sums me up. The square, flat streets, the white houses with their wide porches, the post office in Bailey's Market where old Sally Bunnell passes most afternoons—they're all as much a part of me as my parents and my older brother Daniel.

I know about time from listening to the chimes ringing every hour at the First Methodist Church. I know about respect from walking past Hannah Akeson's place on the way to school. In good weather, she sits on that wicker rocker on her front porch and pesters anyone under the age of fourteen who walks by. "You say your 'Howdy' nice and loud so's I can hear you. Elsewise you might as well not say it at all."

It's the same way with the seasons around here.

I know when they're coming, even before the bunion on Doc Kennett's left foot announces their arrival. In August, the apples in Mr. Peterson's orchard behind our house begin to ripen. Pa checks each morning to see if they're ready for eating yet. Finally, one day he comes home with his pockets stuffed full of Jonathans. He sets them on the kitchen table and polishes each one with Ma's clean dish towel. All the time, he's telling us how he had to sneak the apples right out from under Mr. Peterson's eagle eyes. We laugh. We bite into the red skins. We don't believe a word Pa says, because in a couple of weeks Mr. Peterson will deliver a bushel of apples himself. "For services rendered," he always says. And that's how I know autumn.

Then one night, before anyone realizes Thanksgiving has come and gone, winter shows its face. I wake up just at dawn and hear the wind battering against our windows. When I pull my curtain aside and look out toward the barn, all I can see is white. I hurry back to bed, because I know this first storm is a special one. There's no school in Turner's Crossing that day. It's a tradition. Snow is not that common in this part of Missouri, so they always give us one day to welcome the new season.

Before Daniel went off to the academy in Northridge, I'd sneak into his room on those first-snow mornings. He'd be up and waiting for me. Together, we'd sit on his bed and watch out the back window until the drifting snow lulled us back to sleep. When Ma came in and woke us, I'd find myself curled against Daniel's chest, his arm still wrapped around my shoulders. The imprint of his nightshirt buttons would brand my cheek for half the morning. By the time the marks disappeared, the sun would be out, melting the snow as fast as we could shovel it.

Spring slips into town on the first Saturday in April, just in time for the Apple Blossom Festival. That's when it officially arrives, anyway. Unless of course the festival falls on Holy Saturday, in which case they move the date up a week. When that happens Myrtle Peterson, the chairwoman of the festival, has a conniption fit.

"What if my apple blossoms ain't blossomin' by then?" she complains.

But they always are, frosting the trees with huge white flowers that float to the grass every time even the gentlest of breezes brushes their petals.

"It makes the place look downright springy!" Myrtle says at the annual ham and bean supper that evening. "Can't hardly breathe sometimes, the sight's so pretty."

Then there's summer. In May, Aaron Phelps, owner of Phelps Drug and Emporium, places a big advertisement in the Mid-County Gazette: "Marigold seeds, three packs for a penny. Proprietor has right to limit quantities."

When she sees the ad, Ma always says the same thing. "He's just tryin' to squeeze the last penny out of last year's seeds, though he's got no cause to be that stingy. That man has more money than God." With her next breath, she says, "It must be gettin' on toward June." She's like the minstrels we learned about in history. They went from town to town, announcing the news. Except Ma does her announcing from our kitchen table, leaning her elbows on the bare wood with the paper spread out in front of her.

After Mr. Tubbs, our new superintendent of schools,

started experimenting, I didn't need Ma to tell me summer was coming. Turner's Crossing Elementary used to close in late April, just like the academy and just like every other school in northwest Missouri. That's planting time around here. But Mr. Tubbs came here by way of Philadelphia, where they're a mite more progressive.

"Turner's Crossing is no longer merely an agricultural community," he announced to the school board members. "It has become a bustling center for retail and educational opportunity." Since it was the board members who hired him to begin with, they held his fancy words in high regard. From then on, the elementary school opened in September and ended near the middle of June. It still does. It's not a change I appreciated at the time, but I got used to it soon enough. Just like I'm used to my mother's announcing the news from the kitchen table.

Matter of fact, that's how we first heard about an orphan train coming to town. Ma read the notice to us one evening in May while we were eating supper. I'd been waiting for her usual commentary on Aaron Phelps and his finances, but instead she told us about the orphan train.

"It says right here that they're sending us a group of orphans from New York! 'Wanted!! Homes for orphan children. A company of orphan children under the auspices of the Children's Aid Society of New York will arrive at Turner's Crossing on Thursday afternoon, May 9th, 1905.' "

Pa placed his fork by his plate and stretched his fingers along the edge of the table. "I heard something about that," he said.

My mother looked peeved. "They're not givin' much

notice, are they? And it says here they're going to give away those children at the school hall the very next afternoon. I don't recall anyone sayin' anything about this before."

"It's not been talked about in town a whole lot. They just formed a committee to help place the children. Doc Kennett, Miles Graham, . . ."

"And you?"

"Well, today they decided they needed a lawyer to make sure everything was on the up and up. I told them I'd talk to you about it first."

Ma didn't have a chance to put her two cents in, because Daniel spoke up first. "The whole idea sounds like a cattle auction to me. 'Come one, come all. Best orphans this side of the Mississippi. You got the cash, we got the cow . . . I mean, child.'"

Most times Daniel talks a whole lot funnier than he feels. Everyone in town knows he's as sensitive as a girl about things. His whole life, he's been bringing home injured animals and making them well again. But he tries to hide this sensitive side by making jokes and laughing at himself. He's never fooled anyone, especially not me—or Ma.

"It doesn't seem quite right, standing up before God and man and givin' them poor children away like that," Daniel said, more serious now.

My father puzzled this out in his head for a minute. "Which is worse, bringing the children here where they might just have a chance, or leaving them in the city where they're likely to starve or worse?" he finally said.

"You think like a lawyer, Henry," Ma said.

"You think like a woman, Liza."

"I imagine you already told Doc Kennett you'd be on that committee."

Pa smiled. "You could be right."

The committee, including my father, met the orphan train when it arrived on a hotter-than-the-hinges-of-Hell May afternoon. Right on schedule, the train chugged to a stop in front of the station and deposited its cargo on the platform. It could have been the bonfire on Independence Day, the way so many people turned out for the event. We children had no school. Our classrooms had been made into sleeping quarters for the orphans. Our school meeting hall would be used as a dining room that evening. Later it would serve as "the auction block," as Daniel put it.

Meanwhile, Ma had formed her own committee. "The least we can do is make sure those young ones eat a home-cooked meal while they're here," she told Myrtle Peterson. Once the men finished pushing furniture into place, Ma and her ladies went to work, loading the tables with enough food to satisfy the whole county. Even more rations sat in reserve in iceboxes and pantries all over town.

"Those children will probably be too frightened to eat," Pa ventured, after Ma'd filled his study with pies and cookies that she refused to let him sample.

"You know nothing about children," she told him.

But at the station Ma curled her fingers around my father's arm. "I think you might have been right about all

6

that food," she said. They stood with Doc Kennett and Sheriff Graham. Daniel and I moved closer to the water tower to watch as children spilled out of the passenger car, some of them clinging to each other, some of them crying, all of them frightened by the sea of faces staring at them. Daniel stiffened. I heard him cluck his tongue against his teeth. "Poor little kids," he whispered.

A large woman dressed in too much lace—the kind of thing my mother calls "fuss and nonsense"—scooted the children into a group, arranging them in order from smallest to tallest. Except for one girl.

This one skinny girl, looking worn-out and tired in her limp, red-checked dress, stood in the shadow of the train—not hiding, really, but not joining the other children either as the fat lady pushed them forward. The girl watched the scene with little interest, as if she'd been forced to attend a wedding of folks she'd never met. For just a moment, her eyes flickered over the crowd. Then her mouth set plain in her face. No smile. No expression. No nothing. Hers was the only unreadable face. On the other children's faces you could see both hope and fear. As the crowd surged forward, the children clung to each other, whimpering.

My mother poked my father. I could hear her scolding from across the yard. "Somebody should do something. It's shameful. All those people pecking away at those children the way they are. Poor little things. I got a right mind to say something myself. Then I'd take those babies home with us and feed 'em up proper."

Pa just chomped away on his stogie and watched. Finally, he dropped the stogie and ground it into the dirt.

"You folks got to stand back and let these youngsters catch their breath," he spoke up. "Let's make sure they get their rest, at least until tomorrow afternoon. We'll be sorting out applications at that time." Pushing his way through the crowd, he hopped onto the platform with the children and shook hands with their escort.

"There's only eleven of them," I told Daniel. "Seems like more. There's that one bigger girl with the red dress and then all the littler ones. Must be pretty hard on them. It's hard enough just watchin'."

He didn't answer. I turned to see if he'd heard me. But Daniel had already gone. He'd slipped through the crowd, and I could see him walking down the road, headed for home, his hands shoved inside his pants pocket, his shoulders hunched up around his neck. How I wished I had the gumption to follow him.

People's opinions mattered too much to me, though. I could just hear Evie Durgin sharpening her tongue on my back if I did leave. "You should have seen that Matthews girl, hurryin' down Prospect Street like she was being chased by a ghost. Overly sensitive, you know. Leastways, that's what she pretends. No fortitude is her problem, if you ask me. Not at all like her Mama. It's a downright shame." So I stayed where I was. I even nodded politely at Evie, who nodded politely back.

Pa was still on the platform, separating orphans from gawkers. I didn't realize my mother had joined me under the tower until she started talking. "It'll be better tomorrow, Sissy," she said. Her voice was low and soothing, like she was gentling a nervous horse. "People can't help bein' interested. There's never been such a thing as an orphan train before in Turner's Crossing. Why, even if your father wasn't on that selection committee, we'd be right here in the thick of things checkin' to see what's what, just like everyone else. You can forget worryin' your head about things you can't change."

But Ma didn't understand. I wasn't about to forget. The sight of those frightened children, the memory of that skinny girl and her expressionless face, wouldn't leave me. Not when the fat lady and Sheriff Graham coaxed the orphans into the school. Not when Pa suggested it would be best if we headed on home. Not when Ma broke into the food reserves for our supper. That night I lay in bed and listened to Daniel shuffle around in his bedroom. The whole time I kept thinking, "That orphan girl couldn't be much older than me—maybe fourteen." But she had the oldest eyes I ever saw in a human being. Those eyes troubled my mind long after the chimes of First Methodist sounded out the midnight hour.

The Orphans

P art of me wanted to stay home the next afternoon and help Daniel with the chores he said he'd been neglecting. That's the part of me that pouted when Ma told me she needed my help down at the school. "We'll be making up food parcels to give to any of those poor orphans still left after the selectin', so's they'll have something to eat on the train."

"It'll be just like yesterday—a whole town of people picking over eleven children," I said.

"You'll be mighty surprised to see how few people will be there this afternoon," Ma said. "Not that many folks are interested in taking a stranger into their homes, not even if the stranger's a child."

My pouting hid a curiosity I just couldn't ignore. Even more than I wanted to stay home, I wanted desperately to know what would happen to the orphans. In my mind's eye, I could see the Larsons taking in the smallest girl, a tiny blond with fat pigtails and round cheeks. And I'd bet my mother's cameo that Sheriff Graham and his wife, Agnes, would be looking at one of the younger boys. The Grahams had been married almost twenty-six years—the whole town turned out to celebrate their twenty-fifth anniversary last November—but no little feet had ever skittered down their front steps. "Some kind of woman trouble," Ma said, shaking her head. "Good people like that . . . it don't seem fair. Agnes Graham would make a finer mother than most of the mothers hereabouts."

I worried most about the skinny girl. No one I knew of was looking for an older child. I couldn't imagine traveling from town to town, standing for inspection in front of a bunch of strangers. It'd be even worse to be passed by in favor of younger children, then sent to the next town for the next inspection and the next disappointment. No wonder she showed so little feeling. Such a life would turn the softest heart to stone.

I said all this to Daniel. He was in the barn, cleaning out the mule's stall, and he kept right on working while I talked.

"Pa's right, Charlotte. It's better than stayin' in the city and starvin' to death."

"But it must be so hard—not knowin' what'll happen to you, not knowin' anything about where you're going."

He shook his head. "I don't want to think about that right now, Sissy. I got too much work to do. You best be helpin' Ma pack up all that food she's been hoarding." He straightened up for a moment to ease his back, and it surprised me how tall he'd gotten in the past year. And good-looking. Of course, Daniel's always been better looking than me, even when he was younger and had that owlish look about him. But lately he'd grown into his features. His once-wild thatch of yellow hair had tamed to a more orderly brown. And he looked at the world through eyes as blue and clear as a summer sky.

"I wish you were goin' too," I said. "I don't know how to talk to anyone else."

Daniel patted my shoulder. "It's not so hard as you think, Sissy. Mostly, all you do is say yes or no once in a while and everything will be just fine." That was easy for Daniel, maybe. But not for me.

"I don't see why Jake's suddenly become your responsibility. He's Pa's mule."

"Pa's busy. I'm not."

He'd gotten tall and handsome and responsible all at the same time. I wanted to cry.

Ma was right about there being fewer people in the hall than there had been at the station, but I was right about not knowing what to say. My father busied himself with his committee while Ma laughed and gossiped with hers. I stood beside her and wrapped bundles of sandwiches, cookies, and cakes for whichever orphans would be taking the train on to Trenton in the morning. It took no time at all. We were finished before the fat lady escorted the children into the hall and stood them against the back wall.

"Stand up straight," she reminded them. "And remember, you don't have to go with anyone you don't want to go with. Don't be nervous. These are good people who'll give you good homes."

The skinny girl was the last one to enter the hall. Unlike the rest of the children, she was still wearing the clothes she'd worn on the train. Just like before, though, she stood apart from the rest and watched everything with her old eyes.

Slowly, neighbors drifted in—the Larsons, the Roberts family from Mill Grove, Joe and Evelyn Swindell, Agnes Graham. Miles had confessed to my father that he wasn't sure his wife would come. "She's been disappointed before, you know. Hard to convince a woman to get her heart broke again and again." I almost choked when I saw a sparse-haired woman, her backbone all hunched over, march in like she owned the place. Hannah Akeson was taking in an orphan? But like everyone else, she hung around the entry to the hall, papers in hand, where my father had set up a table and two chairs.

Doc Kennett made the announcement. "All of you here this afternoon are approved homes—exceptin' Miz Matthews and her committee, of course. They're the ones who put out this fine spread here for the children." He nodded to my mother and she smiled. "Miss Frawley, the children's chaperone, can tell you everything she knows about any orphan you might be interested in. Feel free to ask questions. The Children's Aid Society just asks that you provide a good home and a Christian education for the children. It's all on the application. When you're ready, you come set with Henry Matthews here. He'll make sure the paperwork's done all proper and legal."

Daniel was right. This was too much like a cattle auction. I could hardly stand it. I shouldn't have come. I could have pretended I was sick, pouted a bit more, done anything to avoid this horrible scene. It seemed like all the adults were pawing away at the orphans, checking their teeth, their arms, and their legs. They'd finish with one child and move onto the next, poking and prodding until I wanted to scream "Stop!"

But then Agnes Graham spotted a little boy who couldn't have been more than three or four. She knelt down in front of him. "What's your name, honey?"

The little boy's eyes widened, and he swallowed three times before he could whisper, "Michael."

Mrs. Graham took one of his hands into hers. "Michael, would you like to go home with me and my husband? He's right over there—the man with the tummy and the gold watch. He's the sheriff in this town, so he makes sure everyone's safe and sound. Michael, we've been waitin' a long time to have a little boy of our own. You think you might like to be that little boy? We'd take awful good care of you. You'd have your own room and apple pie every day if you wanted it."

That little boy—Michael—wrapped his arms around Mrs. Graham's neck and hugged her so tightly I thought she'd choke.

Right then, I wanted to hug my own father until he almost choked. I wanted to tell him, "You were right about the adoptions after all." But when I walked over to where he sat with Ma, I forgot everything else. All I saw was Aaron Phelps and his wife, standing in the doorway.

No one knew Mrs. Phelps very well. She rarely appeared in public, and when she did, she let her husband do all the talking. Mr. Phelps was a lean, spare man with a look so cold he could freeze an egg frying on the stove. Few people in town actually liked Mr. Phelps, but most respected his business sense. Not my father. Pa had a mighty low opinion of the man, although he never really said why. Ma wasn't so close-mouthed. "Aaron Phelps doesn't believe in paying off his debts. Just ask your father. Why, that man wouldn't give the doctor a cent to save his own wife's life," she said one time. She just about crossed the street when she walked past Phelps Drug and Emporium, and Pa bought our supplies at Hardwick's just outside of town.

Ma spotted Mr. and Mrs. Phelps about the same time I did. She poked my father. "What're they doing here? They don't want a child. All they want is a strong body to do their work for them. They're too lazy to do it themselves. You're not lettin' them take in one of those children, are you?"

Pa didn't have to answer. Doc Kennett took up the challenge. "The Phelps got as much right to a child as anyone else. Maybe more. They own their own home, and Aaron Phelps makes a mighty fine livin' off that store of his. Besides," he said, winking at Ma, "they're lookin' for an older boy. I don't see anybody who meets that description, do you?"

It didn't matter who they were looking for, though. Just like Ma, I mistrusted the way Mr. Phelps smiled at people with his mouth even while he stared right through them with those stone-cold eyes.

The storekeeper spotted the skinny girl right off. He tapped his foot impatiently while his wife looked over some of the smaller children. Then he wrinkled his nose and growled something to his wife.

"What about that 'un over there?" he called to the lady in charge of the orphans.

"Why, I'll be right with you, sir. I was just explaining to this nice couple here the responsibilities involved in taking one of these children. In educating them, in

15

bringing them up in the Lord's way . . ."

Mr. Phelps spat, barely missing the woman's skirts. "I got a store to run. Can't waste my time here all day. You want to find homes for these here children or you want to do a lot of fancy preachin'?"

Something about the way Mr. Phelps looked at the girl made my skin crawl.

Mr. Phelps stood there, hands folded across his chest, waiting to talk with that orphan lady. His wife chirped away beside him until he frowned at her. "Why don't you just tighten that jaw of yours," I could hear him say. It made me so mad that I prayed for courage. "Just once, Lord, I'd like to have gumption enough to do something—to go over there and warn that poor girl."

The Lord must have been in a listening mood. He didn't increase my courage any, but he answered my prayer almost as soon as I said it. Agnes Graham, still clutching little Michael's hand, noticed Mr. Phelps's sudden interest. While Aaron and his wife pushed their way to the front of the line of people, she approached the girl. "You best be going with somebody else," she hissed. "I worked for Phelps for a time when I was a girl. Them Phelps ain't the best for taking care of girls. You'd do better with Miz Akeson right over there." She pointed to Hannah, who was busy inspecting the ears of one of the younger children. "She ain't as fine lookin' as the Phelpses, and she can be downright mean sometimes, but she's good people, as my mother always said. And she's been needin' someone to help her with the chores."

That girl never turned her head once. It was as if she hadn't even heard Agnes. And it was too late anyhow. The lady in charge was coming toward her, propelled by Mr. Phelps on one side and his missus on the other. Her face was beaming as she said, "And I was afraid we'd have a hard time finding a family for you, Jesse Irwin. These nice people have agreed to give you a home."

"I'm already taken," the girl stated matter-of-factly.

Mr. Phelps was not happy. "What?"

The girl stepped out from the wall and stood in front of Hannah. "This lady here, she needs a strong girl to help her, and I'd be glad to be that girl."

Hannah's eyebrows arched and her mouth quivered a bit, but she never blinked an eye. "My! I do like a young 'un who speaks her mind. You ain't so big there, girlie, but you got a strong mouth on you. I do like that, for sure. You heard the girl, Mister Aaron Phelps. This girl here's comin' home with me. Jesse. That's your name, right? Well, Mr. Phelps, you'll have to find yourself someone else."

Mr. Phelps sputtered and fumed. His wife shifted her feet. The fat lady's face turned scarlet, and she wiped her round little hands on her skirt. "It seems we have a problem here," she apologized.

"Ain't no problem here," Hannah insisted. "I want to give this child a home, and she's willin' to come home with me. You ask anyone in town. They'll tell ya I keep as good a house as anyone. I'll sign whatsoever your durn papers say."

I thought I heard my mother's voice say "Good for you, Hannah," but when I looked at her, she acted like she hadn't even noticed the scene Mr. Phelps was creating. Everyone else had, though. It seemed that none of us could do any breathing until the fat lady made her decision.

The woman unfolded her hands and wiped them again on her skirt. Her eyes scanned our faces like she was looking for help. When she didn't get any, she breathed again and said, "It's all settled, then. If you'll just step over here, ma'am, we'll have you sign the papers." I had to admire the lady's gumption.

Mr. Phelps sure didn't. "You're just a miserable fat woman without a husband and family of your own, takin' out your misery on someone else. Well, I'm tellin' you, woman. The people in charge are gonna hear about this. I have rights as a citizen! Ain't no old biddy woman better able to handle a young 'un than me. You just wait. You're gonna hear about this!" He grabbed his wife by the arm and stomped out of the hall.

This time Ma didn't even pretend not to react. "They could probably hear him two counties over into Kirksville with all the ruckus he made."

My father's mouth slid into a smile. He turned to the couples standing around him. "Show's over, folks. Time to get down to business. Who's next?" To my mother, he said, "I think it's about time we headed for home. Let me finish up the rest of this paperwork and we can call it a day."

We weren't the only ones working on leaving. Only a handful of the children had found homes—the small girl with the pigtails, Michael, another little boy, and that Jesse girl. The rest would leave on the morning train. It hurt my eyes to look at such lost faces. Ma dropped her arm around my shoulder. "I know it seems like a cruel thing, Charlotte. But we've done some good today."

I looked up, startled. My mother pointed to Hannah, who was making her mark on the sheaf of papers the fat lady presented to her. "It's a poor sight, all those children being picked over like bones being chewed on by a bunch of dogs. Don't think it's right. But on the other hand, take a look at the Grahams over there."

Agnes and Miles Graham each had ahold of one of their new little boy's hands and were swinging him gently back and forth while they waited for my father to finalize their papers. Hannah and the skinny girl, Jesse, were just leaving. The girl stopped for a moment and said something to Agnes Graham. We couldn't hear what her words were, but we heard Mrs. Graham's answer. "Why that's real kind of you, honey. I'll be remembering that. And don't worry. Like I told you, Miz Akeson here can be a bit cantankerous, but she'll take care of you proper."

"Is that true?" I asked my mother.

"Hannah will do the best she knows how," Ma answered.

Hannah's Charge

Daniel sat at the kitchen table and chomped his way through his second stack of pancakes while Ma discussed the time of day and more. "Agnes Graham looks like a new woman. She's spoiling that little boy of theirs like there's no tomorrow. Can't blame her, though. If I didn't have children of my own, I would've been downright tempted to take him myself." She patted the closest head—mine—and began fiddling with my braids, tucking in stray pieces of hair. "Just tryin' to neaten it up a mite, Sissy. Don't want you goin' to school lookin' like somethin' the cat dragged in."

I sighed. Most mornings Pa would give her a look that stopped her fussing right in its tracks. "I know, I know. I'm just trying to help," she'd say to him. But this day Pa had already left for town. And Daniel was little help. Finally, though, he finished feeding his face long enough to comment, "You hear about Mrs. Spacey and her new baby?" Ma was off again, recollecting how she had known about Alice Spacey's condition before anyone else. "I was first except for family," she added. "Can't hardly blame the girl for lettin' her family in on the secret first."

Ma believed in accuracy, in words and actions.

"I best be gettin' to school," I told her, and slipped out the kitchen door before she could think of something else to bother me about. Instead of me being jealous of Daniel and his extra weeks of freedom, I was grateful to Mr. Tubbs and his newfangled ideas about education. Let Daniel put up with Ma's helpful hints, like I had to do all year.

Besides, I liked school, at least the learning part, and I liked Miss Avery, my teacher. Unfortunately, I was probably the only one of her students who did. Miss Avery didn't have much of a sense of humor, and her mule face couldn't hold a candle to Miss Nolan, the lady who taught school in Turner's Crossing two years ago. My father called Miss Nolan "choice goods," especially in front of my mother, who harrumphed and hurrawed until he chucked her gently under the chin, coaxing a smile out of her. Miss Nolan was also the one who inspired Daniel to write his first, and probably last, love poem. When she moved on, every boy in her class and half of those who had just seen her across the school yard drowned their sorrows in root beer floats down at Hamilton's Ice Cream Parlor.

Miss Avery inspired no such devotion in anyone except me. Even Sara Avery, her own niece, gossiped behind the poor woman's back. "Unsavory Avery," Sara called her, and all of Sara's friends giggled at the nickname. I didn't giggle. I didn't count as one of Sara's friends. But I didn't tell her to keep her opinions to herself, either.

Sara ruled our class as surely as Elizabeth the First

had ruled England, but she was far less merciful. Sara and her chosen friends held all the power. So far, I'd managed to stay clear of her silent treatment, mostly because I let her copy my math homework every morning before school. But once the year ended, so would my usefulness. The way Her Majesty used up friends, I had my hopes, though. I imagined that someday Sara would come begging me for friendship. "Come on, Charlotte," she'd say. "Let's go to Hamilton's for a strawberry fizz. I'm paying." And maybe, just maybe—the third or fourth time she asked—I'd accept. Maybe.

Other hopes crowded my head, too. I wanted to be a teacher like Miss Avery. Well, not quite like her. I didn't want to take my sweet time about marrying the man of my dreams. Miss Avery seemed like she never quite got around to it. Not that she hadn't been asked. A few of the bachelor farmers who needed to start a family had tried, and for a while it seemed like Joe Michaels was going to win her over. But then Joe got drunk as a skunk one night and went carousing all over town. After that, Miss Avery wouldn't give him the time of day. She got mighty particular about everyone else, too. "Too particular," Ma once scolded her. "Sometimes you got to take what the good Lord gives you. No man's worth a grain of salt until some woman gets hold of him and trains him proper."

"You got the only man worth marryin' in these parts," Miss Avery answered. My mother creased her brows and rolled her eyes, but I could tell she was secretly pleased. She, too, thought Pa was the only man worth marrying, and she had been mighty particular herself, hear tell.

Ma had also been "nigh on to beautiful" in those days,

according to Sally Bunnell. "Your Ma was tall and straight and slender when your Pa was courtin' her. And she had that thick auburn hair, like you don't see nowadays. Noontimes, he'd stand right here in front of the window just so he could watch her walk by. He told me she was the prettiest thing he'd seen this side of the Mississippi." My father still thought Ma was the prettiest thing this side of the Mississippi. He told her so all the time. And she was—still tall and straight and slender, still "nigh on to beautiful," although her hair had darkened some.

I doubted that Ma had settled on Pa for his looks. His hair had greyed early, and he wore wire-rimmed glasses that left a dent on each side of his nose. Even in his boots, he stood a good three inches shorter than Ma, so he had to reach up to kiss her forehead when he went off to work each morning. But he had laugh lines around his eyes and mouth, and a way with words that could charm a dog out of its bone. Ma said she was standing in the church saying "I do" before she even realized he'd asked for her hand.

They'd been married in May, like I intended to be. It was my favorite month. Each morning I cut through Standish Cemetery, not because it was the shortest way to get to school, although it was, but because it was the prettiest. Crocuses and hyacinths started the flower show in mid-March. Then came the daffodils, the tulips, and the lilies, poking their way through the damp earth. Finally, Sweet Williams and asters took over, covering the graveyard plots like quilts of many colors, embroidering them with stitches of remembrance. I liked to think about all the sad people who had grubbed in the dirt to plant flowers in memory of those they loved. Every year their flowers bloomed again, paying honor to the dead long after those who planted them had passed on.

You'd have thought it would be quiet in the cemetery, like the inside of an empty church. But the birds, sparrows mostly, stirred up a ruckus as if they were complaining about my presence. They'd soar high overhead, tiny black specks against a crystal blue sky, and I'd have to catch my breath at the beauty of the day. I never told a soul how I felt about the cemetery, not even Daniel. People'd see me climbing over the stone wall and call out, "Seen any spooks lately?" I never told them the cemetery was my idea of Heaven.

That afternoon, sitting in that stifling classroom, I thought twice or maybe three times about how happy I'd been to escape Ma's pestering. With its windows open just a crack, the classroom gave off waves of heat. We wriggled in our seats, our voices droning on and on, buzzing like locusts on a summer's day. We were practicing for graduation—not just the graduates-to-be, but the little kids too, just to keep them busy. Every year, an oratorical demonstration preceded the ceremony. "By the shores of Gitche Gumee / By the shining big sea waters / Stood the wigwam of Nacomus / Daughter of the moon . . ."

Last year the graduates sang "The Battle Hymn of the Republic," but there were eleven eighth graders in that class. This year only Sara Avery, Jonathan Bailey, Richard Frizzell, Betsy Parker, Tom Cunningham, Garth Carlin, Joanna Spencer, and I would be moving on.

"Let's try it again. But this time, I want to hear those

vowel sounds—round your vowels." For about the hundredth time, Miss Avery demonstrated proper lip formation. But a commotion in the hallway caught her in mid-pucker. Before she even had a chance to get to the door, it opened. Hannah marched in, dragging Jesse by the sleeve of that red gingham dress.

This was not the Jesse I had seen at the train station. Gone were her golden curls. In their place, short spikes of hair stuck out at odd angles, like porcupine quills at the end of a dog's nose. The whole class drew back at the sight of her, but Hannah never even noticed.

"We're signin' up for school today," she announced. "Got to do it now, so's this snip of a thing doesn't talk me out of it."

"Now, I don't mind a little ignorance in my house," she explained to Miss Avery. "All a good woman really needs to know is how to read the Good Book and say the Lord's Prayer. But this here girl cain't even do that!" She said this in front of everyone, little kids and all, and I could hear some of the bigger boys snickering. Everyone knew Hannah couldn't read a lick if her life depended on it.

Miss Avery just stared. Her nose wrinkled slightly. The smell of kerosene was stronger than the smell of warm bodies after recess. Miss Avery's reaction must have gotten through to Hannah. "I aim to apologize for the smell, Miz Avery, but I been cleanin' this child up. Makin' sure she's free from bugs and such, if you know what I mean. Good dose of kerosene gets anything that cuttin' the hair don't take care of."

Poor Jesse. If my mother ever hacked my hair the way Hannah had hacked Jesse's, I'd die of shame right

25

then and there. And then to announce it to the whole school besides! But Jesse just stood there, like she was calmly inspecting the students. Her voice carried as well as Hannah's. "I'm not goin' to any school."

Hannah cuffed her on the side of her head. "No back talkin', girl. I ain't keepin' no ignoramuses in my house. Don't want no fancy lady sayin' I don't keep a fit home. I signed my name to that paper. The lady told me I got to git you an education, and git you an education is what I intend to do. Startin' today."

I had to admire Miss Avery's calm. She didn't let herself get all discombobulated. "It's rather late in the year to begin school, you realize." She looked over us students. "I suppose it can't hurt to get Jesse here used to the idea, however. Why don't you sit right over there?" She pointed to a bench in the seventh-grade section. Behind me, I heard whispers of "Cooties" and "Don't get too close." Susan Cunningham moved as far from her new seatmate as possible without falling off the bench. Jesse ignored it all. She marched right over to her place and sat down, with her chin held up right and proper the whole time, like she wore a fancy ball gown and smelled of the finest Paris perfume.

Now Hannah was inspecting the class. She looked up and down the rows, nodding at this child and that one. Her eyes fastened on me, and she grinned toothlessly.

"You Henry Matthews' girl? Your family lives over near the Petersons, don't they? Good stock, those Matthews. I used to be friends with your grandmother, girl." She waved a crooked finger at me. "I see you walkin' to school most mornings. You come over and say howdy sometime soon, hear? I don't want this girl o' mine associatin' with trash. If you know what I mean."

"I'll have to ask my mother," I told Hannah. Ma would say no. At least that's what I would tell Hannah's orphan girl. She wasn't exactly my ticket to Sara Avery's inner circle — and besides, Hannah scared the living bejeezus out of me.

"I knew your mother when she was still messin' her pants. She's got no cause to say no," Hannah shot back.

Jesse smiled, but I don't think she was smiling at Hannah and her foolishness. I think she was smiling because, for some reason, she was happy. Or maybe because she thought she was getting a friend. Of course, she was wrong. I had nothing against her, but I could already hear Sara whispering to her best friend Betsy from behind her literature book. I couldn't help admiring Jesse's spirit. But I also couldn't help worrying about what Sara was saying. It was all fine and dandy if this Jesse person didn't care what other people thought, but I did. And I didn't have to hear Sara's comment about "two peas in a pod" to know who was being discussed, and not kindly.

"How'd the day go?" Ma asked the minute I walked through the back door. She stood at the sink, scrubbing potatoes with a brush. Weaving back and forth through her legs, Cat, my mother's tiger cat, rubbed her cheeks against Ma's stockings. Actually, Cat was a barn cat that spent most of her time finding beds for herself in the hay. But early of a morning and late every afternoon, she made an appearance at our back door, and Ma invited her in.

She'd christen Ma with a head rub, lap up her dish of milk, then meow loudly to go out again. We would have welcomed her to stay inside, especially in winter, but she'd have none of it. Ma said she was too particular to live with people. Pa said she was too particular to live with anyone except Ma, for she hissed even at him—and Pa had a way with animals, like Daniel. It always amazed me that Cat had chosen to bestow her affection upon my mother and not my brother. What amazed me even more was that Ma had such a soft spot for the cat. If she didn't show up for a day or more, my mother would remind Daniel or me to put out a plate of milk for her.

While Ma opened the back door for Cat, I told her about Hannah bringing the orphan girl to our classroom. "Hannah signed her up for school," I told Ma, waiting for her reaction.

"Hmmm" was all she said. Perfect. I could explain the whole day and she'd be too occupied to pay attention, even though she was the one who'd asked.

"Jesse—that's her name. She was wearin' that same old red-checked dress she had on at the train station. You'd a thought Hannah would find somethin' better."

"Hmm."

"Hannah chopped off all her hair. Cooties, I guess. Poured kerosene all over it, too. You could smell that poor girl a mile away."

"Hmm."

"Hannah wanted me to come over and visit, but I said I'd have to ask you. It's not something I'm too keen on."

"Hmm."

I would've bet a live toad that Ma hadn't heard a

word I said. But as soon as we sat down for supper, she repeated my whole conversation—almost word for word—to Pa.

"I got some old dresses and things the poor girl could use, I'm thinking. You can take them over tomorrow after school, Sissy. Hannah doesn't have enough money to buy clothes for herself, never mind any boarder," she added.

"But Ma—"

"That's a good thought, Liza," my father said. "Right kind of you both to help that poor child feel welcome."

Daniel looked up from his plate and grinned. He could nearly always read my mind. I wasn't exactly hankering to be charitable to an orphan girl with no hair, but I shut my mouth right up. No use complaining. Pa spoke real gentle most times, but his word was law in our house. Not because we feared him, exactly. My father took the strap to me only once, and that was because I looked cross-eyed at my mother when she told me to do something. Instead, we respected him. And loved him. And besides, we knew Ma would make life miserable for us if we didn't mind him.

Charity

Nobody said anything to Jesse the next day in school—or the next. She sat alongside Susan Cunningham with her hands mostly folded across her chest. Except when she had to write. Then she grasped her pencil tightly in her first three fingers, and you could see the perspiration seep through the back of that awful red dress. Miss Avery had me collect papers once. The page Jesse handed in was smudged, and her writing was as huge and ill-formed as any second grader's. Miss Avery made no comment about it. She had plenty of comments for everyone else, though.

Every afternoon we practiced "Song of Hiawatha," and every afternoon she said the same thing. "Round your vowels, boys and girls. I want to hear rounded vowels." Jesse moved her mouth as if she knew every word, but not once did I hear her voice.

At lunchtime Jesse sat under the big oak at the back of the school yard and watched. I sat on the school steps with the younger children and watched Jesse. The others spent most of recess following Miss Avery's example— they didn't bother much with Jesse. Every once in a while, one of the girls would hiss "Orphan!" at her, like it was an evil word. But Jesse wasn't easy to rile. She had that look. Even with her spiky hair and ugly dress, there was a certain dignity about her.

I tried to keep my distance, just like I tried to avoid going over to Hannah's with my mother's hand-me-downs. "I only have a little more than four weeks left in school," I explained to Daniel that first night. "I don't want everyone making my life miserable for those last weeks." It made me feel guilty, though.

Discussing my classmates with Daniel took all the mettle I never had. He'd been friends with most of their brothers and sisters. Before going off to Northridge, he and Joanna Avery, Sara's older sister, made cow's eyes at each other across the aisle in Sunday school. He carried her books home from school for her every day of eighth grade. I always thought that was why Sara had not dared to pick on me. Joanna still stopped me on the street some days to ask how Daniel was. Of course, once he was gone, she buddied up to Josh Bailey like there was no tomorrow, batting her eyelashes at him and dropping her hair ribbons on his foot. I didn't tell Daniel that. I didn't have to. Plenty of other folks pleasured themselves by informing him instead.

Daniel didn't get all upset. He had this view of people I could never have. People weren't all good or all bad; they just were. He was like my father that way. Ma called it "that lawyer way of seein' things." Pa was always saying things like, "I don't like to say a man's dumber than his critters, but Josh White should've been born a sheep. Knows all there is to know about corn, though. And he

31

keeps a good barn, clean and full of hay."

It was Daniel who saw Ma clearly enough to remind me of her long memory. "If you think Ma is going to forget about sendin' you over to Hannah's, you're dreaming. Ma's like an elephant. She doesn't forget things, especially when it comes to charity."

He was right, too. I arrived home from school that next day to find a bundle sitting on the back stoop.

"Today, Sissy. You be headin' on to Hannah's with these clothes this afternoon," Ma said the minute I set foot inside the door. "I can't stand the thought of that poor child with nothing decent to wear."

"I'll just put my books away," I started to answer, but I stopped when I got that look. "Now!" it said. There was no arguing with one of Ma's looks.

Through the orchard behind our house, through Gavin Pendleton's back cornfield, I wandered around and about until I came out right in front of the Akeson house. This wasn't one of my shortcuts. It was my protection from Betsy Parker's prying eyes. She lived just around the corner from Hannah, and she spent most afternoons practicing cartwheels in her mother's side garden. I thought it best that little Miss Parker remain unaware of Ma's generosity. Otherwise, who knew what she'd tell the other children. And who knew when Sara's Society might decide to use it against me, to remind me of my place in Turner's Crossing.

If Ma feared that Hannah would be too proud to accept charity, she was wrong. "Jesse girl, you get down here right now. Someone's here callin' on you."

Jesse had barely appeared in the room when Hannah started hustling her back upstairs. "Bring this bundle up to your bedroom, girl. This young 'un here brought dresses from her ma. Just for you. A whole lot of 'em, from what I can see. You get yourself upstairs and try 'em on, why don't you? Save me from dropping a pretty penny at the dress shop come summer."

I expected that my errand would be over once I delivered the dresses, but Hannah pushed me up the stairs right behind Jesse. I followed her down a dark hallway into her room.

One open window, curtainless, lent some air to the tiny bedroom. There was barely enough room in there for two people to stand, so I sat, without being invited, on Jesse's bed. It groaned under my weight, and I sank five inches deep into the mattress. But its quilt covering was as spotless as the woodwork. Hannah was not known for her housekeeping. The change must have been Jesse's doing.

She stripped down to her underwear without so much as an "Excuse me" or "Turn your head, please." Of course, as Ma says, manners don't count too much when you have all you can do to keep your belly from pruning up, so probably Jesse didn't care if I wanted to see her near-naked or not.

And I didn't. Not really. In clothes, Jesse looked skinny as a fence railing. Without them, she looked slender and pale, like the ladies in novels Ma read and then hid on me so's I couldn't read them. She had long limbs and an actual bosom, if you know what I mean, and I couldn't help looking down at my own straight, flat body and being envious.

33

She wasn't so tall as my mother. The first dress she tried on—a muslin with pale blue cornflowers—bunched around her bare feet. A mirror hung on the back of her bedroom door, and she turned this way and that, watching her transformation in the mirror. Slowly, her mouth dropped.

"It looks good. I look good! Well, almost." Near as I could tell, she wasn't bragging about her looks. She just sounded surprised, like the thought never occurred to her before.

"You look fine. Pretty," I said awkwardly. Because she was. In her own way, she was far prettier than any of the girls in Sara's Society. They would not be pleased by this turn of events. Ugly, plain Jesse was no threat. Jesse looking fine in one of my Ma's dresses—that was more than they would be able to handle.

"I never thought about it before. I never realized," Jesse said, turning to me. "It's a truly amazing thing!" That empty-eyed look was gone.

Daniel would think she was pretty, too, I realized suddenly. Like Miss Nolan. It made me proud, this discovery, like I had invented her and couldn't wait to show her off.

"You'll have to wear it to school tomorrow. Or one of the others. Ma sent tons."

That was an exaggeration. Ma had sent over six dresses and one straw bowler. I recognized all of them except one, a faded pink cotton with cutwork embroidery on the collar and cuffs and real mother-of-pearl buttons across each shoulder. Jesse and I saw it at exactly the same time and exclaimed over it at exactly the same time. Then we both laughed at exactly the same time.

All of a sudden I no longer felt awkward. It was fun watching Jesse's transformation from ugly duckling to swan. For the next half hour, while Jesse tried on first one dress and then another, I forgot to worry about how everyone at school would react to this new person.

Later, we sat on Hannah's porch swing, Jesse wearing Ma's pink dress. Her bare feet just touched the floorboards, and every once in a while she'd shove off and we'd swing back and forth slowly.

"I never had such clothes. Not since I was a little girl."

"Your parents died when you were small?" I asked.

"Nah. The orphan train—that's just a name," she told me. "That girl Sara doesn't know anything. We're not all orphans. Me, for example. My mother and father are still alive somewhere. I know it." She said that with a kind of stubbornness, and I could see the muscles in her neck tighten some.

"Do they know where you are?"

I kept my mouth shut, waiting for her to answer. For the longest time, we swung. I thought Jesse forgot my question. But after what seemed like endless minutes, she started talking again, in a voice so quiet it made my ears hurt from listening too hard. She talked like she was telling a story that belonged to someone else, not to her.

It was Christmas Eve. I was sitting in a chair by the window, waiting for my father to come home. He went out to get a nip, as Mama said. It was snowing out, big flakes that looked like puffs of dust. I kept watching the streetlight to see his shadow cross through it. Mama waited with me. We had it all planned. We had my father's present—a vest with real pockets—wrapped and hid-

den. Mama made it out of Grandma's best silk dress that she couldn't wear any more. She'd gotten too fat. The minute my father came home, we were going to surprise him.

Mama and me, just sitting in the chair, my chin resting against the windowsill. Her head was leaning against mine. All the time, those snowflakes were falling, like they were feathers from a pillow, like the snow in the glass globe on my mother's dresser. I loved to shake that. Mama always told me, "Be careful, Jesse. Don't break it. It's a gift from your father." But I couldn't help picking it up. It was magic. Like my father was magic. When he came home, it would be Christmas. He told me I could stay up late, because I would be a big girl this Christmas. I had just turned six.

Mama and my father argued before he went out. I tried not to remember that. "Jack, she's too young to stay up so late. You should have talked this over with me."

"Darlin', nobody's too young to stay up late on Christmas Eve. Remember when we were first married? Remember walking through the park right at midnight?"

Mama's voice sounded more tired than angry. "You always do this, Michael. We're not talking about when we were first married. You're not changing the subject this time. We're talking about a little girl who will have trouble waking up tomorrow morning."

He turned away from her, toward me, and patted my head.

"Now don't you forget to wait for me," he said.

Later, I pushed Mama's angry words out of my head and tried to spot Papa before Mama did, although this was hard. Mama saw things, even in the dark.

We waited—and waited—for almost three hours. At the end of the first hour, Mama tried to make me go to bed, but I wouldn't let her pull me away from the window. I struggled in her arms, so she sat down again, holding me close.

Finally, she stood up. "I'm going to get the police," Mama said. I didn't understand why at first. There was no robber. Nobody was hurt. But then I realized. Mama was afraid Papa wasn't coming home. Not that night.

Not any other night, either. They never found him or what happened to him. For the longest time, Mama was strong. She washed and ironed clothes for people. She sewed dresses with fancy embroidery for babies to be baptized in. The landlady still bothered us, though. And then Mama got so sick. Not the kind where you call the doctor and he gives you medicine. The kind where you can't do anything anymore. After a while, she went to bed. She held onto that glass globe and just rocked, not sleeping, not saying a word, not eating, not letting anyone touch her. She just rocked.

Grandma didn't have much more money than we did, and she was old besides. When she died, they said it was consumption. I took care of Mama after that. Until we couldn't live in our rooms anymore. Even then, I used to find us places where my mother could sleep. And food, too. If your belly is hungry enough, there are ways. I learned every one of them. Finally, though, some people took her away. They told me she died, but I know that's not true. Because she took her glass globe with her. If she had died, she'd have left it for me.

Once, after Mama got sick, I asked her, "What if Papa comes back and we're not there anymore?"

She never answered me. I never had the chance to ask again. But sometimes I think about Papa and wonder where he is. I wonder if he's tucking some other girl into bed and tickling her toes, and making promises to her that he'll never keep.

I didn't know I was crying until I felt the wetness drip onto my neck. "I'm sorry," I whispered, unsure whether I was apologizing for crying or for Jesse's sad life.

"I didn't tell you to make you sad," Jesse said. "I told you because you asked. And so you'll know I'm not an orphan like the other children on the train."

The Visitor

Ma was at me before I got inside the kitchen door. "So, tell me. Did that Jesse friend of yours like those old dresses?"

"She liked 'em all right, I guess." But there was more on my mind than what Jesse thought of my mother's hand-me-downs. I sat at the table, on the edge of my chair. "Ma, if anything ever happened to Pa, what would we do?"

Ma answered plain and quick, like it was a question she thought about every day of her life. "Nothing's going to happen to your father, Sissy. He's healthy as Garth Pendleton's prize bull."

"But what if something did happen?"

She wiped her hands, damp from washing dishes, on her apron, and posed them on her hips. "Why, I suppose I'd teach school, like I always wanted to before I went and married your Pa. Or maybe I'd be a librarian somewhere. All those books, though. I don't know how a body'd get a lick of work done with all those books just waitin' to be read."

I heard her words, but I didn't think about them, not

then. Jesse's story had pushed everything else out of my mind. I needed to escape somehow, to be by myself for a while. "I'm feeling a bit poorly," I lied.

Ma placed her hand first on my forehead and then on my wrists. "You don't feel feverish," she said.

"I just . . . I'm tired is all. It was so hot in school today."

"It's that hair of yours, Sissy. If you'd pull it back instead of leavin' it in braids all the time, you'd feel a mite cooler. Miss Avery and her views on fresh air don't help any. That woman never has the windows open wide enough in that classroom. She's deathly afraid that a breeze might cause consumption."

Luckily, Pa walked in just as she was spouting out words like Ahab's whale spouted water.

"You two relivin' the Lincoln-Douglas debates?" he asked, with a smile for me and a hug for my mother.

"We're just talkin' about things is all," I said. Then I did something I hadn't done for more months than I cared to count. I leaned up to kiss Ma's cheek. As my father's jaw dropped open with amazement, I kissed his cheek, too. Like Reverend Sikes always says, you can't tell when the Lord will be asking for new people in Heaven, so you'd best let folks know how you feel while they're here.

It took me until long after my parents went to bed to decide that I didn't have to feel guilty about not appreciating Ma. I appreciated her just fine. But her endless advice could drive a sane person to the state asylum in Granby. Things could be worse, though. I could be Jesse, all alone in the world but still believing I had parents somewhere who cared what happened to me. That helped me decide. Sara Avery or not, I was now going to be nice to Jesse.

The next morning, ignoring my classmates' raised eyebrows, I greeted her. "Mornin', Jesse." She wore the blue flowered dress. She'd hemmed it, but it was still long on her, almost sweeping the dust, and I heard Betsy and some of Sara's other bosom friends giggle when they saw her. But Jesse in Ma's dress was a force to be reckoned with. She took her place sitting next to Susan Cunningham, and I heard her say to the younger girl, "You've got no cause to fall off the bench like that. I'm not carrying any bugs. Never was." She spoke real soft and gentle-like, but Susan must have heard something in her tone. Susan pushed right in, ignoring Jonathan and the other boys who whispered, "You're gonna get cooties."

I was in agony. Saying good morning to Jesse was one thing. Come lunchtime, I'd have to choose between eating with the little kids, like I usually did, or eating with Jesse. The prospect about scared me to death.

Time goes slow when you're filled with dread. First, Miss Avery spent a whole hour reviewing English grammar for the final exams. "Parsing sentences is the only way, children, that you learn the proper way to write." Adjectives on this line, adverb clauses strung out along the page like a daisy chain out of control. One by one, we went up to the board while the younger children practiced their handwriting. Every time I walked by Jesse, she was struggling with the pen, dribbling ink on her desk and on her sleeve. Sara snickered and poked Betsy. My heart bumped uncomfortably against my chest. It bumped more uncomfortably when Miss Avery made us

41

create get-well cards for Mr. Tubbs, who'd had a boil removed from places best left unmentioned.

While waiting for Miss Avery to approve my design, I snuck a peek at Jesse's handiwork, expecting to see a smudged disaster or, worse, a blank piece of paper. But instead she'd covered the front with fancy curlicues and delicate flowers that could only have existed inside her head. Even Miss Avery commented on her talent. "I'll have to get you started right away designing the invitations for this year's graduation," she said, holding up Jesse's creation for the class to admire.

Twelve o'clock finally came. Miss Avery rang the small bell on her desk. "Lunchtime, lunchtime, boys and girls. Please line up quietly against the board so I can dismiss you."

I made sure I was last in line. Jesse stepped into line behind me. She must have suspected my unease, because she whispered to me, "It's all right."

"What's all right?"

"I don't mind eating by myself. It gives me a chance to think. Figure things out a bit. You eat with your friends." She nodded toward Sara and Betsy

"Friends?" I spoke without thinking. "I don't have any friends."

She thought about that. "Well, then, you have me." Outside, without so much as a how-do-you-do, we sat down on the trunk of the oak tree and ate in silence while the rest of the class watched to see what Sara would do about it.

She did nothing. It occurred to me that perhaps I'd misjudged her reaction to Jesse until I heard her voice above all the others. "My mother says she won't take any of those New York orphans into her house. Why, who knows when they might turn on you and murder you in your own bed?"

"If she's not your friend, why do you let her copy your homework every morning?" Jesse asked me.

I couldn't look at her. Instead, I hung my head and mumbled, "I don't know. I'm just trying to be friendly, I guess." My cheeks must have been purple. "It's just that Sara wants it, and I don't know how to say no without getting her angry with me. Sara's not exactly pleasant when she doesn't get her way."

Jesse shrugged. "You got no cause to be ashamed. You do what you got to do. I've done lots of things in my life I wouldn't tell a soul about, just so's I could get along. Everyone has. But most people make up a lot of nonsense and lies about it."

A visitor showed up on our front porch the next afternoon, right before supper. Before Ma answered the knock, she untied her apron and patted her hair into place. Then she patted mine, just for good measure. We didn't know many people who came to the front door— only Reverend Sikes and Doc Kennett, when they were looking for Pa. I could hear whoever it was passing the time of day with Daniel even before I peeked around the hall corner.

Jesse stood on the porch, carrying a plate covered by a blue-checked towel and daisies tucked under her arm. "Good afternoon, ma'am." Jesse said, as polite as you please. "Hannah sent this plate of cobbler to thank you for the dresses. The flowers are from me—to thank you, too."

"Why that's right thoughtful of you both," Ma said. "You come on in. We're just settin' supper on the table. I'll send Daniel to tell Hannah you're stayin'." She turned toward the kitchen and then stopped. "You look mighty pretty in that dress, Jesse."

I had never known Ma to speak so soft with a body. Almost made me rethink my whole opinion of her.

Daniel got back so fast you'd have thought he'd sprung wings. He followed us into the kitchen. "Sissy says you can draw like a spitfire."

"Sissy?"

"Charlotte here. She's Sissy to us."

Jesse sat at the kitchen table and touched everything on it. She stroked the tablecloth and the plates. Her fingertips traced the scroll pattern on Ma's silverware. All the while, her head bobbed back and forth like a bird's, in constant motion, noticing everything—the rag rug by the sink, the blue enamelware on Grandma Matthews' sideboard, the plain white curtains fluttering in the wind. Cat lumbered in, making her daily begging stop, and Jesse stooped low to touch her fur.

"Cat's not exactly friendly to anyone except Ma," Daniel warned her.

But he was wrong. That cat curled around Jesse's hand like the girl was made of catnip. First she rubbed her forehead along Jesse's thumb. Then her whole body wriggled through Jesse's fingers.

"You got a nice way with her," Ma said. "She's pretty particular about who she likes. But she's a good momma cat. She's got a litter of kittens out somewheres in the barn. When they're old enough, you can take one home."

"That'd be real nice, Mrs. Matthews." She pretended to be composed about it, but her eyes danced with excitement. "How old do they have to be?"

"Eight weeks is best. And if'n I'm remembering right, Cat had her kittens a couple or three weeks ago. That's when she lost her belly, anyway."

Pa stomped through the back door, raising enough dust in the pantry to choke a skunk. He paused in the doorway when he saw Jesse. Ma, smooth as glass, introduced our guest without making any special fuss. "This here's Jesse. She come to bring us Hannah's special cobbler, so I invited her to stay for supper."

My father was downright gallant. He wore no hat, but he pretended to tip it anyway. Then he took her hand and shook it. "Nice to meet you, Jesse. Charlotte has told us so much about you."

I snuck a look at Ma. Her eyebrows were halfway up her forehead. I had said very little about Jesse, preferring to avoid the subject whenever possible in case Ma got it into her head to be charitable again. But now that Jesse was here, sitting in our kitchen and smiling shyly at my father's fancy manners, I was glad. And proud. I wasn't quite sure why.

Ma had me walk Jesse home after supper. "It's the polite thing to do," she hissed when I opened my mouth to complain. The sun had just set beyond the ridge, and the peepers were out full force.

"I never saw such a flat land," Jesse said. "No real

hills, no mountains, no nothing. Except those bumps of land way off in the distance. It's like you could see clear through to tomorrow if you wanted to."

"Not all of Missouri is like Turner's Crossing. That's what Daniel says. He's been to the state capital with Pa, and one summer he traveled straight through to Hannibal to visit Grandpa before he died."

"Did your mother mean what she said about the kitten?"

"Ma doesn't say things she doesn't mean. If you want to, we can try to find them in the barn tomorrow. Although it won't be easy. Cat usually hides her babies pretty well under the hay," I said.

"Cats make the best mothers in the animal kingdom," I told her. I was quoting Pa without thinking about what I was saying. "They're even better than humans. That's what my father always says when he wants to tease my mother." Then I stopped short, remembering that Jesse might not want to hear about good mothers.

But Jesse didn't seem to notice. "Maybe I'll come by tomorrow to see if we can find those kittens. Can't remember the last time I saw a kitten."

"Ma won't mind if you come," I assured Jesse. At least I didn't think she would. I'd never put her to the test before because I'd never had someone I could invite to my house before.

"You have a nice family," Jesse said sleepily. "Nice father. Nice mother. Nice big brother."

The windows in Hannah's house were dark. You'd expect Hannah to leave one light on, to help Jesse find her way upstairs. But maybe Hannah didn't know any better.

I worried aloud to Pa after I arrived back home. He was sitting in the living room on the rocking chair, smoking his pipe and reading the newspaper. "Do you think Miz Akeson will do right by Jesse? Take care of her well enough?"

"Seems to me that girl is smart enough to do a lot of taking care of herself."

"Hannah didn't even leave a light on in the window for her."

"Miz Akeson doesn't have gas lights like we do, Sissy. She can't hardly afford paying taxes on her property, never mind wasting her money on lights."

"You would have lit a candle for me. To make sure I got home safe."

"Not everyone's family is like ours," he said.

I knew he was right.

Kittens

We were setting down to breakfast the next morning when Pa came through the back door. He soaped up his hands at the sink and scrubbed them until they were pink. Without turning, he addressed my mother.

"Seems like old Jake got that cat of your'n. The durn mule stepped on her. Must've happened sometime last night. She was just lying there in his stall. I buried her out back."

My mother's face froze. She'd always pretended that Cat was just like any old barn cat that meant nothing to her, but there were plenty of signs that said different—the way Ma made sure there was enough cream left for the cat, the way she stroked the creature's silky coat, even the way she cottoned right on to Jesse when Cat took a liking to the girl. Pa placed his arm around my mother's shoulder. "No use gettin' all sudsed up over it. She was just a cantankerous old barn cat," he said, but his voice was tender.

Ma shook his arm away. "It's not that. She had kittens that were still nursing. Did you see them?"

"Not a whisker, darlin'."

"I hate to think of any creatures starving to death. After breakfast I'll go out and see if I can find any of them. See if they're still breathing."

"I can do that for you, Ma," Daniel offered. He'd already galloped through his breakfast, so he headed directly out to the barn.

Search as he might, my brother didn't find the kittens. I told Jesse that before school, so she'd not be expecting one of Cat's babies.

Jesse thought she was fooling me. She acted like she'd barely heard what I said. I never saw a body pretend to be so completely uninterested. She almost yawned when she asked, "What'll happen if you do find them?"

"They'll be dead, most likely. But if they're not, Pa'll probably drown 'em. They die quick and easy that way."

Her indifference vanished in an instant. "No!" she shouted. "He can't do that!"

I looked up, startled by the explosion.

"I mean . . . I know I could find them for your mother," Jesse said. "Seein' how she's so attached and all, it's the least I can do to thank her for givin' me those dresses."

"I don't think she's that attached. She just doesn't like to see creatures suffer. And even if we found them, I don't think it's easy to raise orphan kittens," I told her.

"It's been done, though."

I shrugged. "Don't know as how we've ever tried it before. Ma would know best."

My words must have sounded so ignorant to Jesse. Of course she didn't want the kittens to die. They were orphans, just like she was. She wanted to take care of them, the way no one had ever taken care of her.

That afternoon in the loft, partway under the eaves, Jesse and I found Cat's nest. There were three little babies, barely warm to the touch. Daniel had followed us out to the barn. He looked at the limp, tiny bodies and shook his head, but Jesse was too busy inspecting the kittens to notice.

"We ought to bring them inside," she said. "It's damp in here. They need to be warmer."

"We can try, I suppose," Daniel said. He scooped one into each hand. Jesse cradled the smallest kitten in her palm. It had a white throat and three white feet. Tabby markings were beginning to show through its grey coat.

"I never saw anything so tiny," she said, like she was talking to herself.

The kitten she held squirmed this way and that while my brother inspected its tail. It was the only one that showed any signs of life. "That's a little boy, I'm thinkin'," Daniel told her.

Jesse rubbed her chin across his body. "This one's the pick of the litter," she said.

Daniel tried to explain. "He's very weak, Jesse. They all are."

But I don't think Jesse heard him. She was too busy warming the kitten with her hands, treating it like it was the king of England. I hoped like anything that Ma could save it.

Ma took charge. She heated a pan of milk on the stove, then filled an eyedropper with the warm liquid. Just like she was caring for a baby, she rolled up her sleeve and tested the milk on the inside of her forearm. She took a kitten in one hand and pried its tiny mouth open with the eyedropper. Quickly, she forced the liquid inside. The kitten sputtered and choked. The milk dribbled out through its mouth and nose.

We sat around the kitchen table, taking turns filling the eyedropper and trying to force-feed the kittens for what seemed like hours. First one kitten, then the next. Jesse wouldn't let go of the little tiger she was holding. Every time her fingers grasped the dropper, she'd square her jaw and her mouth would set straight in her face. "Now you swallow this. It's good for you. It'll make you strong." She spoke to the kitten like he could understand every word.

Long after Daniel straightened up and said, "This isn't working," Jesse kept trying to feed the little animal. She rubbed its belly and murmured to it, then plunged the eyedropper into the milk, squeezed the bulb, pried open the kitten's mouth, and squirted the milk inside. Again and again and again. Her dress was soaked. The milk was almost gone, and the kitten's eyes had glazed over. Finally, my mother placed her hand gently on Jesse's. "I think it's enough, Jesse. Even if you got him eating now, who's to say it would work the next time?"

Jesse raised her head. "Just a little while longer. I know I can do it. I just have to try a little while longer."

"Honey, the other kittens, they're dead. It was too soon for them to be away from their mother. I think this one's gone, too. Jesse?"

Jesse pulled her hand from my mother's grasp. "I need to do this. Please."

My mother hesitated, then nodded. "You do what you must, girl." We all watched as Jesse again dribbled milk on the kitten's lips.

"Swallow the milk, little cat. Swallow it now!" she commanded.

Suddenly the kitten's throat contracted. His eyes focused on Jesse, and he licked his lips. Then he angrily dropped his jaw and screamed.

From that moment on, Jesse couldn't feed him fast enough. As soon as she placed the milk in his mouth, we'd see him swallow and he'd open his mouth and scream some more. We watched him guzzle milk until his tummy rounded up, and finally he closed his blue eyes.

"Now you have to rub his belly like this," Ma said. She had a damp cloth, and she gently drew it across the kitten's damp fur.

"To wash him?" Jesse's whole face puckered like she had eaten a lemon.

Daniel laughed. "In a manner of speaking. At least to clean out his innards. We're just helping him do what comes natural to you and me. That's what a momma cat does, too, to teach her baby how to take care of himself."

"What about the others?"

Ma shook her head. "No. We'll have Sissy's father bury them next to their momma under the lilac bushes. Daniel, you go get one of those wooden crates from the barn. Mind you, get two. We can use one to make a bed for this little one here." Daniel scooted out the door, letting it bang behind him.

For a while we sat there, watching as the kitten curled itself against Jesse's chest. With her long fingers, she stroked his body from his ears to the very tip of his tail. He purred softly at first, then as loud as any train chugging into the station.

"There's nothin' sweeter than a sleeping kitten," Ma said. I had to admit she was right. All the flowers in the cemetery and all the apple blossoms in Myrtle Peterson's orchard couldn't compete with the sight of that sleeping baby with his soft white chin and his lips partly curved into a smile.

"This kitten will be all right," Jesse said.

"It'll need a lot of feeding," Ma cautioned.

Jesse tried to sound unconcerned. "I don't know if Hannah knows anything about cats, but I could bring him home with me and try to feed him for you."

"Why don't we do this," Ma proposed. "If you promise to come here every morning and after supper every night for the next few weeks, we'll keep the kitten here. I'll take care of him during the daytime. Or Charlotte here will."

"So somebody will be here the whole time to make sure he's all right?"

"We'll keep an eye on him."

"Then, when he's bigger, you'll have another cat for the house."

Ma smiled. "No, Jesse. This kitten is yours. Remember? I promised you one. Besides, you saved his life."

Jesse's fingers froze. She squeezed her eyes shut. "You promised me? I didn't think . . . Mrs. Matthews, I'm grateful to you."

Ma's eyes misted over some. Mine, too, if the truth be known.

"You'd better wrap him in this old towel here. We'll

put him by the stove while I'm cooking supper to keep him warm."

Daniel clattered through the kitchen door, carrying the crates. He placed one on the floor nearest my mother. The other he held out to Jesse. "You lay him right over there, next to the stove. Don't squeeze him to death. Lord, girl, you got to give him a little air to breathe." Anyone could see that Jesse was having a hard time letting go.

I watched as Jesse and my mother made a bed for the kitten. For an instant, I was jealous of how easily Jesse seemed to fit into my family. In the next instant, I felt guilty. My whole life, Ma's mothering had vexed me. Now that she was mothering someone else, I resented it.

"I'm sending you girls to Phelps Drug and Emporium," Ma said. She poked inside her apron pocket for change. "Fresh cow's milk—that's not the best thing for a kitten. I've got some evaporated milk in the cupboards, but we'll need some elixir, too. The medicine they give foals to spice 'em up should do about as well as any other kind."

"Phelps?" I asked. She'd never once sent me there before.

Ma gave me her look. "Hardwick's doesn't carry such a thing. Your father will understand."

"But Daniel could do it."

"Daniel and I have other things to do." Her eyes met his across the table, and for a moment his face was blank. Then, slowly, he nodded. Might have known. Ma wouldn't leave unpleasant work for Pa to deal with. She'd take care of it herself, with my brother's help. I felt sorry for him, but I knew I'd rather face Mr. Phelps straight on than stay here and bury those poor kittens.

I had a hard time keeping up with Jesse's long strides, but it was even harder to keep up with her train of thought. "Hannah will be thinking I got kidnapped or something. I probably should have stopped by to tell her I'd be late. I never knew cow's milk wasn't good for cats. I thought that was all they drank."

"I can't believe Ma would let me set foot inside Phelps Drug without her or Daniel there, too," I told her. "She doesn't like Mr. Phelps one bit. And my father. If he ever finds out, he'll probably skin me alive!"

"But your mother said it was the only place they have the right kind of medicine."

"That won't matter. He'll still skin me. Pa doesn't cotton much to Aaron Phelps."

And I couldn't blame him. The man acted like a snake. There is no other word. He smiled when he saw me walk through his door. His smile got even wider when he saw Jesse walk through his door.

"Well, well, now. What have we here? Two fine young ladies. Lookin' for something for your Pa, are you?"

I shook my head.

Jesse didn't act the least bit uncomfortable. "We're here to pick up supplies for Mrs. Matthews."

Mr. Phelps wagged his finger at her. "I got a good mind to hold a grudge against you, girlie. You bamboozled my wife and me. But I ain't one to stay angry. You tell me what you're lookin' for, and I'll see if I can 'commodate you."

Jesse spoke right up. "Mrs. Matthews needs the kind of medicine they use to keep young horses healthy."

"Easy enough," said Mr. Phelps. He started fussing

around behind the counter. "You and Hannah gettin' along, are you? I see you're lookin' all spruced up and pretty in your duds there." His head was bent low behind the shelves, but I swear I could hear his teeth grind when he said it.

"Well enough," Jesse answered. "We're learning each other's ways."

He straightened right back up. "Well, you remember, girlie. Any time you get enough of that old woman, my wife and I are lookin' for a girl, and we ain't found one yet. The wife sets a mighty nice table. And we hire out for any hard scrubbin'.""

He deposited the bottle of elixir on the counter. "Since when do you Matthews got a foal?"

"We're not buying it for horses. We need it for a kitten that lost its mother."

"Well. That's downright thoughtful of you two girls. Takin' care of a little animal like that. Nothing like a cat in the house to make it feel all warm and cozy-like. Tell you what. You take this bottle for free. On the house, like they say in the city."

I opened my mouth to protest, but Jesse was already thanking him for his generosity.

"Just doin' my part." He wiped the spotless counter with a spotless rag. The whole time, he kept right on smiling. Suddenly I couldn't look at that smile any longer. It seemed as false as Sam Lawson's new teeth. I walked past Jesse and out the door.

"It's not a good idea to take charity from that man," I said when she joined me outside.

"He was trying to be nice."

"Ma says the day Aaron Phelps does something nice for anyone is the day he's found a way to make a million dollars off being generous. And I don't like the way he looks at people. He looks like he's in league with the devil himself."

Jesse didn't smile. "I've seen the devil himself many times, and I'm tellin' you, Charlie, he didn't wear Mr. Phelps' face. At least not so's I'd recognize it."

I was right about Ma making Daniel bury those other kittens. When I got home, he was sitting on the back stoop, his head bent inside his arms. He lifted his head when he heard my footsteps, and I could see streaks of dirt lining his cheeks like Indian war paint.

"Thank you for helping save Jesse's kitten," I said awkwardly.

He shrugged. "Didn't do much. Ma did most of it. And Jesse." For a moment, I could hear the excitement in his voice. "Did you see that, Sissy? The way that kitten suddenly came to life in her hands? Just like magic. It was like sometimes when I'm treatin' some animal and I know suddenly, without question, that they trust me—only me. I never met anyone else who could do that."

I recognized his tone. Last time I heard it, he'd been talking about the way Joanna Avery's shiny brown curls bounced every time she laughed. Before that, he'd been talking about how Miss Nolan smelled of lavender refresher, and how it was the sweetest perfume on earth.

Daniel was developing a fondness for Jesse. I wasn't at all sure how I felt about that.

Max

Jesse was as good as her word about coming over every day to feed that kitten. For the next couple of weeks, she arrived just at dawn. After slipping through our back door, she'd gather the ingredients for Max's first meal of the day. That's what she named him, Max.

My parents were already up. Pa liked playing the gentleman farmer. He spent the first hour of every day feeding and cleaning up after Belle, Ma's sweet-faced, shorthorn cow; Xavier, our sow; the chickens; and Jake the mule. Ma fixed Pa's breakfast and hers while she waited for him to come in from the barn. Most mornings, the smell of coffee and the hum of my parents' voices drifted upstairs and woke me. I'd lie in my bed, reluctant to part from its comfort, until my father summoned us to breakfast.

Daniel could sleep through a cyclone twirling around his bed. Many's the day I anointed him with water from his wash basin, only to have him turn on his other side and sleep on. The first few days after Jesse found the kitten, however, we both got up early. I wanted to enjoy the novelty of actually having a friend; my brother just wanted to enjoy the sight of her. But after a couple of mornings, I got tired of watching Daniel watch Jesse. Besides, I discovered that getting up at dawn meant my mother found more things for me to do. So I hid in my room until she sent Pa calling for me.

After sloshing water on my face and hands, I'd descend the staircase in my bare feet. The scene that greeted me was the same every day. Ma stood at the kitchen table, kneading dough for the day's loaf of bread; Jesse was hunkered down nearby. In her lap sat Max. Her hands stroked his fur, unconsciously dusting away the flour that had settled on him after my mother's too-vigorous mixing. Daniel'd be sitting next to Jesse, his chin resting on his hands as he listened to their chatter. And there was always laughter. Sometimes Ma made comments about the kitten's weight and energy, like she was an interested friend of the parent. "He's gettin' on there in size, missy. In a few days, we'll try mixing scraps with the milk and see what he does."

Just as seriously, Jesse would answer, "He's certainly growing faster than I expected."

If my father was there washing up at the sink, he'd chuckle to himself. "If I didn't know better, I'd say these here womenfolks were talkin' about a growing child, not some pesky feline."

Every morning Ma said, "We'd be pleased to have you eat breakfast with us, Jesse."

Every morning Jesse responded, "No thank you, Mrs. Matthews. I still got things to do before school." She'd hand Max to me carefully, like he was her greatest treasure on earth. "I best be going. But I'll be back after supper."

And she was.

Most of the time I loved having a friend, especially one who fit in so comfortably with my family. When the two of us were alone, we talked about everything and nothing at all. She didn't seem to mind my silences; I appreciated her worldliness. Only one thing bothered me. Jesse was supposed to be my best friend. I was the one who discovered her. But sometimes, watching her with my mother and Daniel, I realized that she no longer belonged just to me.

Ma and Jesse were more like mother and daughter than Ma and me were. My mother never harassed her about her clothes or hair, and I could hear the pride in Ma's voice when she discussed "that poor orphan child" with her friends. "Why, that girl is the most responsible human being I ever met in my life," she'd proclaim. "Solid. Like stone. That girl's going places, I tell you."

And ever since Jesse saved Max, my brother acted like he'd discovered her all by himself. Once, he interrupted Max's feeding. "Jesse, you want to hold my raccoon for me while I clean out his wound?"

I followed them out to the barn. The pens for Daniel's creatures took up most of the back wall. One housed a squirrel with half its tail shot off. Another was a temporary home for a couple of baby foxes. Lucas, the raccoon, had his own quarters, and an injured snake hid itself beneath the hay in a wooden crate.

Lucas didn't need much holding. He sat on his behind, chirping and chattering like he was gossiping with Sally Bunnell outside Bailey's Market. He didn't even move when Daniel started cleaning his front paw with water and Ma's carbolic soap.

"It took Daniel three days before Lucas here would let him touch his paw," I bragged. "But he's right at home now."

"That's because he trusts you," Jesse told Daniel. She ran her hand along the raccoon's back. Lucas flinched for a moment. His eyes inspected Jesse while he shook water from his paw. Then he began chattering again.

Daniel grinned. "You have a nice way with animals yourself," he said.

Jesse turned her head a little, as if his words embarrassed her. But I don't think she really minded, the way she let her mouth relax into a smile. "You'd better pay attention to that raccoon of yours," she warned Daniel. "He's about to tip over the water bucket."

Daniel reached for the bucket, but he was too late. Water splashed over him, his raccoon, and the clean hay. He was still scolding Lucas when Jesse and I slipped out the barn door and back to the house.

"A little attention sure makes that girl blossom," Ma commented at supper. She was right. Jesse acted like a bud that had finally received enough sunlight, and most of the sunlight came from Ma and Daniel. She ignored Daniel's teasing, but her cheeks pinked right up every time he spoke directly to her. I tried to remember that Jesse had nobody, that Hannah didn't know how to give her the time of day. But it stung to listen to my mother sing her praises and to watch Daniel nod happily at her every word.

I couldn't hate Jesse for any of it, though. I admired her

too much. She was the sister I always wanted and never had. I loved the way she acted so fearless, and the way she stood up to everyone, especially Sara and her society.

One afternoon at school, while we were reading *Ivanhoe* out loud, Susan Cunningham couldn't control her upset over poor Rebecca's death sentence. "It's not fair!" she kept repeating. "Does she get rescued? Does Ivanhoe save her?" Her crying tortured our eardrums for over half an hour. Miss Avery did nothing to comfort her. The ruckus she raised was bad enough for Sara to decide that the younger girl was on the outs with her and her friends.

It didn't help that Susan was one of "those" Cunninghams, the dirt-poor farmers who lived outside of town and came to school with bare feet. Her brother Tom, sixteen, would be graduating this year, even though he hadn't been in school since April. He and boys like him were what the townspeople called "Mr. Tubbs's casualties." Each spring they left school to work in the fields. As a result, they never received credit for attending a whole school year. But this year the school board had seen fit to reward Tom's longstanding persistence with an eighth-grade diploma.

I was glad. It pained me no end to see him disappear each planting season. I worried that someday he'd quit school like his father before him had done. Tom had the softest brown eyes and the longest lashes I ever saw on a human being. He treated me with a gentle courtesy that set my stomach fluttering every time he drawled, "Morning, Charlotte Ann."

Sara, on the other hand, made a lot of noise about a

farm boy being allowed to graduate, and she treated Susan like the girl was dirt under her fingernails.

"Little Susy Crybaby," she hissed that day behind Miss Avery's back.

Jesse walked right up to Sara after school.

"You shouldn't be doing that to Susan."

Sara pretended shock. "Doing what?"

"Picking on a little girl like that. She wasn't hurting you. You shouldn't be hurting her."

I thought Sara was going to keel over dead right then and there. I thought her friends would, too. Instead, Sara just sashayed away, like a queen bee followed by her swarm. But I noticed that she didn't torture Susan the next day. And although she tried halfheartedly to make comments about Jesse, the best she could come up with was, "Pushy white-trash orphan. Who does she think she is, Miss High and Mighty? With her background?" Which was pretty useless, seeing as how Jesse didn't care one way or the other what anyone thought. At least she didn't seem to.

I was surprised that Sara didn't start in on me.

"She needs your math homework too much," Jesse said as we walked through the school yard. "And she needs you to help her on final exams."

I had been helping Sara on math tests for years by keeping my elbow out of the way of her roving eyes.

"She can't see that far," I lied, knowing perfectly well that Sara had the eyes of an eagle when it came to stealing other people's answers.

"It's nothing to me," Jesse said. "I told you before. I done too many things myself to be judging others."

I could feel the tears stinging at my eyes. "But it makes me ashamed," I whispered.

"Then that's why you have to stop. Because you're ashamed."

It was easy for her to say. But I knew I'd never have that kind of courage.

It amazed me to no end that Jesse chose me for a friend. Maybelle Adams's nature suited her better. In seventh grade, Maybelle stood taller than my father and was twice as broad. She was the only one of my classmates to ever get into a fight with Sara—a screaming, hair-pulling spectacle that happened one recess in fifth grade. Sara stayed pretty much out of Maybelle's way after that. In fact, everyone stayed out of Maybelle's way after that, mostly because she told us to. She'd say hello to Jesse on occasion, though, and once or twice I saw them talking before school. But it was me that Jesse sought out each lunchtime, and me that she waited for each day after school.

Evenings, Jesse and I sat out on the back stoop and waited for Max to finish eating like a pig. There are no other words to describe how he ate. He entertained us by pouncing on June bugs, crawling up our legs under our skirts, and chasing fireflies around until he toppled over. He protected us from all sorts of imaginary dangers, like twigs, puffs of dust, and shoelaces.

"It's like watching a whole motion picture show performed by one tiny creature," Daniel said on one of the nights he joined us. He would know. Northridge Academy was close to the big city, where they had such things. "I saw *The Great Train Robbery* twice last spring, but it wasn't near as interesting as watching this little guy's adventures."

Daniel vied with Max for Jesse's attention. He told stories about sneaking out of the library on Saturday afternoons to see vaudeville performances. He teased me mercilessly about my cleaning habits—or lack of them. "The living room rug sets four inches off the floor 'cause Sissy here keeps sweepin' the dust under it." But Jesse didn't give him much more than the time of day. She was too busy keeping watch over her kitten. Not that she needed to. Even after dark we rarely had to look for Max, because his purr penetrated right through the shadows. Daniel said it best. "He's got a purr louder than Pa sawin' wood in his sleep."

After she finished the supper dishes, Ma often joined us. She'd take her apron off and wipe her hands on it. Then she'd sit on the stairs with us and let the cool evening air dry the sweat from her forehead.

One night, when Pa borrowed Daniel to help him replace the boards that Jake had kicked out of his stall, she sat on the bottom step, where my brother usually sat. She raised her skirt up to her knees and let the breeze fan her legs. "Had to get outside for a breath of fresh air," she said. Then she turned to me. "I've been thinkin'. You'll be graduatin' in just a few short days, Sissy."

"She's got the best grades in the whole school in math and science," Jesse told her.

"That I know. Bright as a penny, right from the time she was born. I used to watch her forehead crease up when she was tryin' to figure somethin' out. Like when she was watchin' a bug on the wall, or learnin' how to walk. Sissy never did bother to crawl. She just up and decided to walk one day. Never a how-do-you-do about it."

I could feel my cheeks redden, but it didn't matter. Ma's tone had that same note of pride I heard when she talked to other women about Jesse. But then she ruined the whole thing.

"Purpose, though. That's a different thing. You got to be developin' a goal in life somehow, Sissy. You're too smart by half, but you got to want somethin' bad enough to go for it."

Jesse interrupted. "What do you want to do when you get out of school, Charlie?"

I didn't have a chance to answer.

Ma grasped my braids and rolled them around her hands. "Why, she could be anything she wants—a lawyer like her daddy—even a doctor, seein' as how she's so good in science."

"Ma!" I protested.

My mother put her arms around my chest and hugged me until I could hardly breathe. "I've been thinkin'. We got to do something special for such a bright shiny penny, don't you think, Jesse? What about a party? A little party for Sissy and you and some of your classmates."

"I don't want a party, Ma."

"Nonsense. Every young girl wants a party. It would be no trouble at all. We can invite that Avery girl and Betsy Parker and some of the others."

"Sara Avery won't be coming to any party of mine," I told her. "Please, Ma. Just Pa and you and me and Daniel and Jesse. I don't want anybody else."

"But honey, think of the fun you could have."

All of a sudden, I couldn't stand it any more. "It wouldn't be any fun at all!" I shouted.

I left her and Jesse sitting on the stoop and ran into the house, taking the stairs two at a time. I raced into my bedroom, slamming the door behind me, and flung myself onto my bed. But it hurt too much to cry. We had been doing so well. For a few moments I had heard what I'd always wanted to hear in my mother's voice—pride. Then it was gone.

In a little while, I heard someone knocking very lightly at the door. It would be Ma. She would be properly sympathetic. I would be properly apologetic. We would hug and pretend that everything was all right.

"Come in, " I told her.

But it was Jesse's face that peeked through the door. She slid inside, closing it behind her, and sat next to me on my bed.

For the longest time, we said nothing.

"She doesn't understand anything," I told her at last. "How it is at school."

"No, she doesn't."

"She has so many friends. She always did. I can't be that way."

"It's all right."

"And I can't tell her. If I told her I didn't have anyone, that nobody liked me, she'd be ashamed of me."

My tears, once started, dripped onto my cheeks and my hands, soaking through my shirtwaist. But I couldn't stop crying.

"You know your mother loves you."

"It's not the same. Parents have to love their children. I just don't want her to be ashamed of me. I don't want her to know I don't have any friends. I'd be so humiliated."

"But you have friends. You have me."

It made me cry harder. This poor orphan girl without anyone in the world was comforting me, a person who had everything.

"You should have been Ma's daughter, not me," I said suddenly.

"That's nonsense." Jesse sounded angry.

"It's true. You two are so alike, so strong. And I'm not. I'm always afraid. You and Ma, you're not afraid of anything."

"You're wrong about that. Everyone's afraid sometimes. I'm afraid. Just like your mother and father and Daniel are afraid. Just like everyone is. It's not something to be ashamed of. It's how you act when you're afraid that matters." She handed me a handkerchief from her skirt pocket. "Here. You need to wipe your eyes before your mother sees you. She feels real bad about upsetting you."

My voice was filled with wonder. "She feels bad because of me? She said that?"

Jesse actually smiled. "She's a little close-mouthed about such things, but I could tell."

We dangled our feet over the side of the bed for a while without speaking. All the time I couldn't help thinking, "Jesse's awful prideful. Not the way Reverend Sykes means when he preaches that pride goeth before a fall, but she never lets anyone shame her for any reason. Maybe that's why Sara didn't pick on her. Maybe that's why Daniel admires her so much."

Suddenly I wanted to ask her, "Do you know that Daniel thinks the sun rises and sets on you?" But brothers and sisters have to protect each other's secrets. So instead, I asked, "Is Hannah good to you, Jesse?"

Her face clouded over, and her hands pleated the folds in her skirt. "She's the best she knows how to be, Sissy."

She let herself out of my room without saying another thing. I dried my face on the hand towel by my nightstand. Her words seemed to echo in the room: She's the best she knows how to be.

Like Ma was the best she knew how to be. Maybe I expected too much from my mother. Maybe I wasn't being fair. I wanted her to understand me, but I never had the courage to tell her the things that would help her do just that.

Graduation

"Sissy, you should have asked me to tie this sash," Ma told me. "You got one of the streamers wrinkled already, and we haven't even left for your graduation yet." I didn't remind her that Pa made the bow, like he always did, smoothing the loops against my back and straightening my collar at the same time. When I was small, he'd pat my behind when he was finished, but I'd become too much of a lady for that, leastways that's what he said.

Ma's words didn't bother me, though. I felt too good. My white eyelet dress made me feel like a princess in some fairy tale. I twirled the skirt and watched my reflection in the hall mirror. For the first time, my hair was up. Ma had wanted to curl it into ringlets and let it hang down my back, which would've made me feel like a hoity-toity model in the Sears catalog. But a couple of afternoons before, Jesse had piled it all on top of my head. "It looks best that way," she said. Even Daniel agreed. Although Ma did a bit of grumbling about it, she gave in. She complained, though. "I wasn't allowed to put my hair up until I was sixteen years old."

Even that couldn't rattle me. I was graduating. From Turner's Crossing Elementary School. Me!

I could remember being in first grade and counting on my fingers how many years it would be before I got to wear fancy white eyelet like the graduates. My father was the speaker that year, and he told us about how leaving school didn't mean you left learning behind. He told about how Ma would read his law books right alongside him so he'd have someone to study with. It was the only time I saw my mother with actual tears on her cheeks, and I thought maybe she stuck herself with a pin. Daniel told me different. "She's proud of Pa. That's all. Sometimes people cry when they're happy more than when they're sad."

"I can't get over how pretty the invitations are to this shindig," Pa said for the tenth time as he turned the card over in his hand to admire the artwork.

"I told you Jesse was a good artist," Ma said, also for the tenth time. The invitations were Jesse's doing. She'd drawn a different cover on every one. Sara's had butterflies dancing around a field of daisies. Mine had a rose bush with just the nose and whiskers of a kitten peeking out from beneath it. Betsy Parker was so thrilled by her invitation with its cover of black-eyed Susans that she whispered to me, "I don't think orphans are any trashier than half the other people in Turner's Crossing. But I wouldn't say so to just anyone."

Jesse had come by the house early, bringing some violets for me to wear with my dress. She placed them in a glass of water. "I took them from the back yard. Hannah doesn't even know they're growing out there. They'll look

71

fine on you when you stand in front of everyone to receive your awards."

"You going to graduation?" Daniel asked.

His face fell when she told him, "It's not likely. Hannah thinks it's a lot of foolishness. 'Didn't have sich nonsense when I was a young 'un, and I ain't about to condone it now,'" Jesse said, imitating Hannah perfectly. "Anyhow, I haven't been in school long enough to learn the recitation."

Her mimicry made us giggle, but I turned the rest of her excuse over in my mind. Not true, I thought to myself. She knew the recitation as well as I did. I'd watched her lips move when we practiced it on the stage. Miss Avery had her sit in the back of the hall, to make sure we sounded loud enough. Then we'd practiced going up to receive our diplomas. "Remember to shake the superintendent's hand properly. Don't forget to say thank you. The same goes if you get an award. Walk slowly up to the podium and shake hands with your right hand."

Miss Avery hadn't announced who would receive awards, but it was pretty much expected that I would receive special notice in science and math. Betsy Parker would be awarded a prize in literature, and probably history, too. Only one award was really in doubt—the Most Deserving Student Award, given each year to the eighth grader that most exemplified ideal deportment and generosity of spirit. Sara Avery figured she had dibs on that one. I could tell by the way she smirked to her friends when her aunt discussed its importance.

Sara wasn't speaking to me. I heard her hiss to her society when I walked up to practice shaking hands with

Miss Avery. But it didn't matter. She was just smarting because I hadn't let her copy my answers on the math exam, and her test had come back with a big fat red F across the front page. Only her mother's begging and Sara's earlier passing grades allowed her to participate in graduation. When I thought about her now, I wanted to laugh. Free! For eight years, I'd suffered under that girl's spell, but at long last I would be free of her. Sara had no intention of going on to high school. "I have better things to do," she said.

"She's too stupid to go to high school," I crowed one day after school.

Jesse frowned. "That's not very nice."

Her criticism surprised me. "She's not a very nice person. Especially to you."

"I'm not too smart either, you know."

I hadn't known, and I didn't believe it. It never occurred to me that Jesse could think that way about herself. It was true that she had trouble writing things down. And she stumbled over every other word when Miss Avery asked her to read out loud. But I never thought of Jesse as stupid. She was the smartest person I knew. I told her that.

"But I can't hardly read. And I make so many mistakes when I try to write."

"That's because you haven't had much schooling. If you had the same schooling as me, why, you'd be head of the class."

"All the same, it bothers me when people call other people stupid." She paused for a moment, then her mouth curled into a smile. "Besides, I was counting on her graduating. When she flunked her math examination, it bothered me no end. I thought for sure she'd be sitting right beside me next year, picking on that poor Cunningham girl all over again."

That very morning we older students had transformed the school hall into what was probably the fanciest space in all of Carroll County. It looked like a garden someone had dug up and planted indoors. Pots of geraniums filled the windowsills, and sprays of pink and yellow roses decorated each row of chairs. Miss Avery had Jesse create garlands of lamb's ear, statice, and baby's breath. The sixth and seventh graders tied the garlands across the front of the stage and around the top of the podium. Ten chairs— eight for the graduates, one for Mr. Tubbs, and one for Miss Avery—sat on the stage.

That evening I waited with the rest of my classmates at the back of the hall and watched my parents march between the rows of chairs. They found seats right down front, close enough to the stage to touch it. I was embarrassed, but a little proud, too. Pa nearly burst the buttons on his vest, and even Ma forgot to pester me about anything after she re-ironed my sash and tied it herself. They saved a seat for Daniel, who'd be late. He'd stayed behind to feed Max, who reminded us right as we were leaving that his stomach was empty. Daniel'd have to slip in the side door and find his seat beside Ma just as Mrs. Plimpton pounded out "Pomp and Circumstance" on the piano forte.

Too soon, the hall was crowded with friends and relatives and younger students who chattered easily together, filling the room with a comfortable buzz. For a moment, I felt envious. I wanted to be one of those people just jawing away about nothing at all. Where'd they ever find so many words to say to each other? Why couldn't I ever think up those words? But just before we lined up to march down the aisle, Tom Cunningham touched my shoulder and said, "You look pretty, Charlotte Ann." I thought my insides would about melt.

His compliment helped me survive the ceremony and the recitations after. Our whole class rounded our vowels well enough on "Song of Hiawatha" to please Miss Avery. Then Betsy Parker stood up and placed her carefully cupped hands in front of her. "I will be reciting 'Captain, My Captain' by Walt Whitman," she announced. It was a brave choice. Miss Avery had warned her that a poem about Abe Lincoln might not be well-received in these parts. But Becky was sure it was the right selection. Her head waved back and forth dramatically on the last line of each stanza.

There were some hisses in the audience. Gramps Loughlin and his kin were from Ozark country, and they didn't take too kindly to the poem. They still refought the War Between the States amongst themselves every evening, and they managed to defeat those "durn Yankees" at least twice a week. But most people in Turner's Crossing appreciated Becky's efforts. As she swept her arms across her brow on the final line of the poem, folks clapped politely. Doc Kennett followed, speaking about higher education and how it could improve your lot in life.

Then it was time. Superintendent Tubbs stood at the podium and withdrew a sheet of paper from inside his coat. In a gravelly voice that carried back to the far corners of the hall, he announced the awards. First the science award: "For excellence in the pursuit of scientific investigation, this award goes to Charlotte Ann Matthews." Then the mathematics award: "For excellence in mathematical solutions and problem solving, this award is given to Charlotte Ann Matthews." The leather bottoms on my new boots skittered on the polished stage as I walked across it to receive my awards. Ma'd be after me for that. She'd told me to scuff up the bottoms before I wore them. Each time, however, my luck held, and I made it up and back safely. "Next time I'll listen to her," I thought as I landed thankfully in my seat.

Betsy Parker was on my right. Just as I thought, she received special notice for English and history. After receiving her awards, she sat down with a thud, shifted in her seat, and sat down again, this time on my dress, half strangling me in the process. I could hardly breathe. Then Miss Avery replaced Mr. Tubbs at the podium and made the special announcement.

"Every year we award a prize for a student who shows the most generous heart, the student who has contributed most to our class by his or her example to others." Sara Avery sat there wearing a smug expression on her face. She was so sure of herself. All of her friends were, too.

"This year the Most Deserving Student Award goes to Charlotte Ann Matthews."

I stood up. My dress did not. *Rrrip*. I could hear the tearing sound as I rose, but it was too late. In my proudest moment, I was about to be humiliated in front of the whole audience. Quickly, I pulled at the dress, yanking it out from under Betsy. I walked up to the podium, clutching my torn skirt, feeling every eye on me. "They're all watching me, laughing at me," I thought. I shook Miss Avery's hand and took the plaque she offered, barely remembering to say thank you. Then I returned to my seat. My body slumped in the chair, and I tried to hide my face behind the program. "Everyone saw," I thought. "I looked like a fool."

Those were the first words I said to Pa after graduation. I handed him my prizes—the plaque, two dictionaries, and *The Natural History of the State of Missouri,* and tears spilled onto my cheeks. He didn't try to convince me otherwise. He just took me into his arms and hugged me tightly to his vest. "Do you know how proud we are of you, Sissy?"

My mother patted my back. "No one even noticed whether your dress was torn or not. They were too busy honoring the best student in Turner's Crossing."

But it was Daniel I believed. Brothers don't lie about such things. "White dress, white underthings. Who could even tell?" he said, squeezing my hand.

I laughed, and that made me choke through my tears. All at once I was laughing and crying at the same time, and I had no idea if I was happy or sad, proud or humiliated.

We got home late, after punch and cookies and those fancy cakes called petit fours that Ma always made for special occasions. Jesse was waiting for us by the back door.

"I thought Max might need his supper. And seeing as how you've all been so busy, I didn't want you to bother yourselves about him."

"He's been fed, Jesse. Daniel here did it while we were walkin' Sissy over to the school," Ma said. "But you can always give him a little more. He's a growing boy. Mix a little leftover peas with the chicken this time. Mush it up real good, though."

Mindful of my mother's admonition to keep my dress clean, I stood on the back stoop while Jesse sat. Garth Pendleton had cut his back field that afternoon, and the sweet aroma still hung in the air. "I love the smell of just-cut hay, don't you? I've been smellin' it my whole life and I don't think I'll ever get tired of it."

"You had a good graduation?" Jesse asked.

I thought about my torn dress and the recitation and the awards. "It was just fine," I said. "The hall looked wondrous. I never saw a sight so pretty. My family commented on it highly, especially my brother. And Tom Cunningham said I looked nice." I waited for a moment. "I tore my dress. Betsy Parker sat on it, and it tore when I stood up." I showed her the damage.

Her words echoed Daniel's. "I wouldn't even have noticed if you hadn't pointed it out. Your petticoat fills in the rip."

Max finished his second supper, and just like a baby with a full stomach, he found the most comfortable spot to sleep it off—Jesse's lap. Her eyes weren't old when she looked at him. They crinkled at the edges with pleasure, like Daniel's did when he looked at Jesse.

"Do you like Daniel?" I asked her, suddenly brave.

She sounded surprised. "Like him? I suppose so. Why?"

The relief in my voice must have been obvious. "I was just wondering. That's all."

"He's a nice boy, Charlie. But he's too young for me."

"He's three years older than you are."

"Years don't mean anything. Sometimes I think everyone in the world is younger than me."

Lying in bed that night, I started thinking about my Most Deserving Student Award. Generous heart. Contributed most to the class. Set an example. It all sounded more like Jesse than me. Next year Miss Avery would find her classroom easier to manage, and not just because her niece wouldn't be there. It would be because Jesse had standards that people wanted to live up to. People like me. Next year she'd be graduating—she was smart enough to catch on to writing and reading—and she'd look a whole lot better in her white dress than I did in mine. She'd receive the Most Deserving Student Award, and they'd just have to give her one for art, too. Hannah would sit in the audience and clap for her, like my family did for me. That's if Hannah would even let her go to school next year.

I fell asleep worrying about that, and about whether Tom Cunningham noticed my torn dress, and about so many other things that I could have counted worries like most people counted sheep.

The Rainbow

A few days after graduation, Ma asked Jesse and me to pick wild strawberries for her. She bribed us by saying, "I'll make a couple of pies, maybe more dependin' on how many baskets you fill." I didn't need to be bribed. Looking for berries gave me an excuse to spend time with Jesse. Max was growing so fast that he really didn't need special feedings any longer. Soon he'd be old enough to go home with Jesse, and I figured that would bring her daily visits to an end. Besides, this way we'd have a chance to escape from Daniel and his puppy-dog expression. He didn't give up easily, though. "I can help pick the berries," he told Ma. "It'll go much faster with three people."

But Ma shook her head. "Daniel, with your father working so late on Matt Campbell's land case, I need you to finish his chores as well as your own." I didn't wait around long enough to see if this new adult Daniel sulked like the old one had. The summer was short, and too soon I'd be traveling to Northridge to high school. Spending time alone with Jesse was too precious a thing to pass up.

We searched the banks that ran alongside the

railroad tracks for the strawberries. Jesse had never sampled one, so she dropped the first berry she found into her mouth instead of the basket. She looked like she'd just swallowed a live tadpole. "You sure these are what your mother wants us to pick? For pies?"

"It's actually a mite early to pick them for eating purposes. But Ma likes the tartness, and she adds a fair amount of sugar, so they taste different when they're cooked down. Besides, Ma uses 'em for more than pie. Usually she makes strawberry cordial with them."

Ma had warned me that very morning. "This is the summer," she said. I didn't have to ask what she meant. She hinted at the same thing every year. She wanted desperately to teach me the recipe for cordial, just as it had been taught to her by her mother, and just as her mother had learned it from my great-grandmother. But such things didn't interest me much, and I could never understand why she wasted so much time making a sweet liqueur that she wouldn't even sample. Both my parents were teetotallers. Like other good Presbyterians, they never imbibed anything stronger than grape juice, even on New Year's Eve. But Ma liked to give bottles of strawberry cordial away at Thanksgiving and Christmas. Pa always teased her, and she'd bristle like a rooster. "Not all of my friends are Presbyterians," she'd remind him sharply. "Some of them like to serve a fancy drink on special occasions."

"How do you know it tastes right?" Daniel asked her once.

Her lips pursed together. "Oh, I know. There's an art to it."

There's also an art to berry picking—pick three, eat two. But if you're picking on an afternoon so hot it feels like your back is frying right through your blouse, nothing matters except finishing up.

"Have we got enough yet?" Jesse wanted to know.

I peeked inside her basket. "I suppose. But it takes a whole lot of berries to make both pie and cordial."

Jesse didn't normally show much emotion one way or the other, but right then she closed her eyes and wiped the pools of sweat off them with the heels of her hands. "This must be how it feels to die and go to Hell."

"We can always pick more tomorrow if Ma needs 'em," I said. "Or the day after." I couldn't quite contain my happiness. "Just think. We're free! No more school for the whole summer!"

"No more Tom Cunningham, either," Jesse teased.

"I don't care." I'd already decided that he had just been acting polite. I appreciated his words, but I wasn't going to hang an engagement ring around them. "It's summer. Finally!"

Right on cue, summer spoke up with a crash of thunder. Unfortunately, the storm caught us just as we were traipsing through the fields behind Peterson's orchard. "Get down!" I shouted to Jesse.

She looked at me with frightened eyes.

"Get down," I repeated and pulled her down into the hay.

The whole sky lit up, and the earth trembled under our bodies. "Jesus God," Jesse swore.

"Haven't you been in a thunderstorm before?" I asked, shouting to be heard above the roaring wind.

"Not like this one!"

We didn't say anything for a while. The noise of the storm was too loud. After the crashes of thunder, the rain came, pelting down on us, stinging our backs and legs. For what seemed like forever we lay in the field, waiting for the storm to pass. I could see Jesse's lips moving. I swear she was praying.

Then, just as suddenly as it began, the storm eased up. No more flashes of light accented the thunder's anger. The rain sputtered to a gentle dripping. We lay there for a few minutes, still not saying a word. I listened to make sure the rumbles were traveling on toward Monroe and wouldn't turn back around on us. Slowly, the rolling sounds faded and the dark clouds broke.

"I should have watched the clouds more carefully," I said as I sat up and squeezed the rainwater from my hair.

Jesse's white face stared at me. "It was like the Last Judgment—fire and brimstone."

"It was just a thunderstorm," I said. "Look quick. Up in the sky. Maybe we'll see a rainbow."

Her face began to gain color. "Rainbow?"

"In the sky. It happens when the sun reflects on the raindrops. You know." I pointed to the sky. "A rainbow."

"I know what a rainbow is," Jesse said. Then I heard her sharp intake of breath. "Jesus God," she said again, but this time her voice sounded prayerful. "I never saw anything like that before." Through the parting clouds, a pale arch of colors curved across the entire eastern sky.

"You never saw a rainbow?" I was shocked.

"Not since a long time ago. They don't have many rainbows in the city."

"Maybe people just don't bother to look for them."

"Maybe people just don't have the time. Maybe they're too busy scrambling, just trying to survive." There was a trace of bitterness in her voice. Or maybe it was sadness. I wasn't sure which.

We lay on our backs and watched the rainbow brighten as more of the sun broke through. Then, slowly, the sky cleared. The colors melted into each other and disappeared.

"Doesn't last very long," Jesse observed.

"Pa says it lasts only as long as we need it to."

Pa was silent when I told him about Jesse and the rainbow. He had come into my bedroom to kiss me good night, like he did every night, but for the first time in a long time I wasn't pretending to be asleep.

"That girl's led a hard life, no doubt about it," he said.

"I'm glad she's with Hannah instead of Mr. and Mrs. Phelps. Aren't you?"

He hemmed and hawed like the lawyer he was and finally said, "I guess it does make me feel better."

He'd been working hard on the Campbell land case for over a month — one brother was fighting another over thirty-eight acres of cornfield — and his whole face looked weary and discouraged.

"I think Ma wants me to be a lawyer or a doctor when I'm older," I told him.

"Or a candlestick maker? Indian chief? Baker? That's because your mother thinks you can do anything you set your mind to, Sissy. She's got a lot of grand ideas for you."

"But they're not really my ideas. What about you, Pa? What do you think I should be?"

"I think you should be anything and anyone you want to be."

"You know what I'd really like? I'd like to be like Jesse—not an orphan, not like that, but the way she is, so sure of herself. I'd like an ounce of her gumption."

"Sissy, you've got a good brain and a kind heart. You're just fine the way you are. Besides, it's not good to be admirin' Jesse too much."

Try as I might, I could not get him to explain what he meant. He meant nothing bad, though, I could tell. I think he was trying to say he didn't want me to have to live a hard life. He liked Jesse just fine, respected her even. I could tell.

"I'm glad Jesse was with you when she saw her first rainbow, Sissy."

"Why?"

"Because other people might not have even bothered to look up in the sky." He kissed my cheek and ruffled my hair. Softly, he let himself out of my room and closed the door behind him.

Like Ma, I thought after he left. Ma was too busy fussing with things on the ground to look up and see rainbows.

Ma wasn't seeing any color but red the next morning. "That woman!" she fumed. "I'm too much of a lady to call her what she deserves to be called."

Pa's eyebrows joined together on the top of his

forehead. "Liza, you're not speakin' ill of your neighbors, are you?"

Daniel stifled his chuckle.

"I'm speakin' about that intolerant, insufferable Delia Avery. Sara's mother. It's no wonder that girl acts so highfalutin and fancy, with a mother like that."

"Darlin', somethin's got you all riled up. You talkin' about Delia Avery stealin' recipes from people and not givin' credit where it's due, like she did last spring?"

"I'm talkin' about how that woman is having a birthday party for her precious Sara on the evenin' of the thirtieth, and she's inviting most all the young people in Turner's Crossing. Exceptin' Sissy and Daniel won't be able to go."

"That's just fine with me," I said.

"I'm not sayin' you weren't invited, Sissy. I'm sayin' you aren't going."

My father tried smoothing the waters. "Is there any reason for this?" He sounded puzzled. He wasn't the only one. After all the times Ma tried to force me to be friends with Sara and her society, I couldn't believe she was rejecting a chance for me to attend one of Sara's command performances.

"Mrs. Avery said, and I quote, 'I ain't invitin' no orphan children to be at my Sara's party. I don't believe in invitin' people just to be polite. And I especially don't want my Sara surrounding herself with girls like that Jesse. Who knows what trash she comes from?' I told that woman it'd be fine with me if Sissy was friends with a hundred Jesse Irwins. Jesse has real manners—not like Sara Avery with her simpy 'Yes, ma'ams' and then gossipin' about people behind their backs."

Pa grabbed her by the waist and rubbed his cheek against hers. "You are some woman, Liza Matthews. You truly are. I'm right glad I cottoned on to you."

Ma blushed and scooted him away. "You're going to be late for court, and you better not be tellin' Judge Evans it was because you were flirting with your wife, like you did not long ago. I couldn't show my face in town for a month."

He kissed her cheek. "I promise. I won't tell anyone ever again that I flirt with my wife. I'll just tell 'em we . . . ," he paused dramatically, "we overslept."

She shooed him out of the kitchen with her dishrag.

Daniel's ears were bright red, and he wouldn't look up from his plate. I couldn't tell if he was trying not to bust out laughing or if he was embarrassed by my parents like I was. At the same time, I admired Ma's sticking up for Jesse. I'd probably have been afraid to do the same. But I didn't know how to say I appreciated what she'd done. We'd been talking at cross-purposes for so long that I had no idea how to tell her much of anything. All I could do at the moment was eat everything she put on my plate without complaining. I even pretended to listen when she complained about the state of my hair and the wrinkles in my dress. But after my third helping of ham and eggs, Daniel looked at me quizzically.

"You feelin' all right, Sissy?"

Ma's ears perked right up.

I kicked his leg under the table. "I'm just fine. Just tryin' to keep up with you."

Ma busied herself wiping the top of the stove and

scrubbing the fry pan. The whole time I was working up the courage to say something. But it was hard. Finally, just as I hurried out of the kitchen, I muttered under my breath.

"I'm sorry, Sissy. You got to speak up. Sometimes you mumble so a body can't hardly hear a word you're saying."

My patience had worn out. "Thank you, Ma," I said, in my loudest and most impatient tone.

I didn't tell Jesse about Sara's party. Mrs. Phelps did instead, although she didn't mean to. We'd gone in the store for Max's final bottle of elixir, and she asked me right out: "Your mother planning on buying you a dress for the Avery shindig, or are you wearing your graduation dress? Reason is, Mr. Phelps is having to order a lot of dresses for this here party, and I don't want anyone complainin' they had to wear the same dress as someone else."

"I'm not going to Sara's party," I told her.

Mr. Phelps, standing by the back of the store, said in his too-hearty voice, "What's this I hear? A party bein' held and you two ladies not a party to it?" He laughed at his own joke.

"I'm just lookin' for one last bottle of that foal elixir so's we can finish feedin' Jesse's kitten, Mr. Phelps. We'll take a nickel's worth of peppermint sticks, too." Ma had given me five cents more than we needed, telling us to buy something sweet with the extra. She was still feeling badly about Jesse being left out of Sara's party.

Mr. Phelps motioned his wife aside. "That I can do

you for," he said, and counted ten sticks onto the counter. He wrapped the candy in brown paper. Then he grabbed two more out of the jar. "What the hey. Here's two extra sticks. On the house, as they say." Jesse thanked him graciously. I merely nodded.

"Come in anytime, girls," he said, but he wasn't talking to me. It made my skin crawl, the way his eyes never once left Jesse.

"You can go to the party, you know," Jesse said later, as we dipped our bare feet in the pond back of Hannah's house. She was sitting on the grass beside me, with her profile turned toward the light. The summer sun had streaked her short hair almost white, and I could see the resolute set of her chin.

I didn't pretend that I didn't understand. That was a game you played with the Sara Averys of the world. Jesse deserved better.

"I don't want to go," I told her, meaning every word. "Neither does Daniel."

"He said that?"

He hadn't, not in so many words. What he had said was, "That Avery girl and her kind. Why, Jesse's worth more than all of them combined." But I couldn't tell her that. He'd have knocked me down dead.

He'd also offered a suggestion. "We ought to take her to the carnival the afternoon of Sara's party. It would be lots more exciting than watching a bunch of girls clucking away, anyhow." Daniel said this lightly, but I couldn't help noticing how eager his face had looked when my mother agreed.

We had things planned for after the carnival, too, Ma and Daniel and me. We'd give Jesse a tea party with some of Ma's special little cakes and maybe a pitcher of her lemonade. Then, just before Jesse left, we'd present her with Max, all done up in a ribbon and bow. It might not be as fancy a to-do as Sara's party, but I knew that wouldn't matter to Jesse. She'd have Max. I couldn't wait to see her face when she realized that her kitten was coming home with her for good.

The Carnival

J esse and I sat on the front porch that very next afternoon, sorting through strawberries for Ma's cordial recipe. Max entertained himself and us by batting one of the rejected berries across the floor and skittering after it. He didn't care if he had to barrel right over a body's toes to chase it, so I kept my feet tucked under my skirt. Slowly, I worked the idea of going to the carnival into our conversation.

"They're setting up the tents right outside of town, on the old Northrup place. They do it every year, and the town council gets pretty riled up about it. 'Can't see why that carnival has to come to town so close to Independence Day every gosh-darned year. People haven't a dime in their pockets by the time we hold our own shindig,' Doc Kennett always complains. But my parents don't pay him any mind. They're lettin' Daniel and me go all by ourselves this year. You think you might want to come along?"

Jesse didn't show any great interest in going. She hemmed and hawed and tickled Max's tummy with her bare feet while she decided. Maybe city folks don't get the same pleasure out of squandering an afternoon that country folks do. Or maybe they think there's better places to spend their money. Or, just maybe, Jesse didn't know what a carnival was.

Daniel popped his head out the front door and grabbed a fistful of strawberries before I could smack his hand away. "You going with us to the carnival? Ride the carousel? Grab a gold ring? Maybe even win a prize?"

Jesse perked right up. "Prizes?"

"Prizes. And a Ferris wheel bigger than this house, and cotton candy and games of 'No-Chance,' as Pa always says." Daniel sounded like a carnival barker selling his wares.

"I guess I wouldn't mind seeing all that."

Pa played at being shocked. "Liza, you mean you're lettin' your children go alone to that den of sin and iniquity? Lettin' them take that poor unsuspecting city girl, too? I can't hardly imagine that, darlin'."

Ma poked him. "You best be watching your tongue, Mr. Smart Matthews. That girl just might decide to high-tail it off with one of those smooth-talking carnival men. How would you like to explain that to the Children's Aid Society?"

"Jesse's got a whole lot more sense than that," I said.

Ma smiled. "That's a truth. Besides, Daniel here'll be along just to make sure there's a little competition."

Daniel's cheeks reddened right up, but he was much better than me at handling awkward moments. "Who's going to protect me from those hoochy-coochie dancing girls they hide in the tents until after dark?" he joked.

It was Ma's turn to blush. "You're getting awful big for those britches, Mr. Daniel. What do you know about hoochie-coochie girls, anyway?"

Daniel smiled like he had swallowed a whole nest of canaries. "Oh, Ma. I can't be tellin' you all my secrets. Don't want you worryin' none when Sissy goes off to the academy with me come September."

She opened her mouth to reply, but snapped it shut instead. She and Pa must have had words about me going off to high school, and she wasn't about to tell us what they were.

The morning the carnival opened its gates, Daniel and I walked over to Hannah's. Jesse sat on the porch waiting for us. She wore Ma's faded pink dress, carefully ironed. Her hair had begun to grow out, and it framed her face with tiny curls that clung to her forehead and wound around the tips of her ears. She looked pretty as a picture, and Daniel told her so without so much as a quiver in his voice.

Jesse ignored his compliment. "I need to be home before supper," she informed me.

Daniel didn't act put off any. He leaned against the porch railing, his legs crossed, his arms folded across his chest. He had that glimmer in his eyes, like when he was trying to coax a smile out of Ma.

"Is that those Matthews children?" Hannah called out from the kitchen. She came to the door and shoved it open. "That you, Charlotte Matthews? Your brother, too?"

"It's me, Miz Akeson. And Daniel."

She looked Daniel up and down. "Well, now. You're a

mite beyond bein' a child, aren't you? I hadn't quite noticed. Last time I saw you all spit-and-polished like this, you was wearin' knee pants and suspenders."

"That was three years ago, Miz Akeson. You were in black silk and white lace cuffs. At your brother's funeral. Remember?"

She checked his face to make sure he wasn't being disrespectful. Then she smiled. "That's right. You and your daddy were there, payin' respects. I think kindly on that. You got your father's charm, boy. Just make sure you don't be using it on my girl here. And make sure she gets back before it's time to cook supper."

Tension seemed to build in Jesse's body as we walked along. She held her arms tight against her sides, and her breath came in spurts. It was like she was about to bust wide open—like Cinderella must have felt going to her first ball. I felt like the fairy godmother, but I couldn't decide who Daniel was. He was either Prince Charming in disguise or one of those mice that got themselves turned into footmen.

He strolled along in front, hands shoved in his pockets, and whistled some tune I didn't recognize. When he wasn't whistling, he kept up a steady stream of chatter that I barely paid any heed to. His attitude toward Jesse puzzled me. He didn't seem to mind that she ignored him, but I would have sworn on my grandmother's Bible he was holding out a torch for the girl.

When we were about halfway there, it finally struck me. Daniel thought of Jesse as one of his injured creatures. He figured that, given enough time and enough gentling, she'd start to trust him like those wild animals did. "Not this time," I wanted to tell him. "This time, all the taming in the world might not be enough. Jesse's just finding her way in the world. She's not even considering romance. Besides, she thinks you're too young for her."

Past Phelps Drug, past Hamilton's Ice Cream Shop. We didn't have to walk much farther to reach the carnival. The closer we got, the more my stomach churned with anticipation. My heart started pounding hard against my chest, and my fingers danced against my skirt. Finally, like a castle appearing out of nowhere, the carnival came into view.

It spread across Northrups' pasture as if Merlin had cast a spell, turning the field into a place so magical that I caught my breath at the sight of it. Towering over everything else was a huge Ferris wheel that alternated between spinning on its axis and sputtering to a stop to pick up new passengers. But there were other sights to behold, too. Games of chance and gypsy fortune tellers and all sorts of food booths crowded the Midway. Along each side were booths offering the major vices—gambling, drinking, and dancing—but these would stay covered until the evening, when the adults came calling.

It smelled just the way I remembered, like burned candy and sweat. It sounded the same way, too—noisy. A calliope competed for attention with carnival folks who hawked their wares by shouting at everyone who walked by. The whole place was dirty and loud and altogether too thrilling. I snuck a look at Jesse to see if she felt the same way. Her face revealed nothing, but her feet just couldn't keep still. She kept tapping them against the ground, like she was a dancer tied to one spot.

"You wait here. I'll get us some tokens," Daniel said. He took our nickels and disappeared into the crowd.

The minute he left, Jesse questioned me. "Tokens — are they for those prizes Daniel was talking about the other day?"

"No. They're for the carousel, the Ferris wheel, and the other rides. If you go on the Ferris wheel, though, you have to pay an extra token."

Like a child admitting some misdeed, she whispered, "I've never been to a carnival before."

"I've never been to one without my parents."

Daniel returned with one hand full of tokens and the other hand carrying three boxes of spun sugar. "Fairy floss, just like they served up at last year's Exposition," he said. He handed one to each of us and watched as Jesse reached in and took her first careful taste.

Her eyes widened with astonishment. "It's like nothing I ever ate before!" she said.

We laughed. She frowned for a moment, as if she didn't appreciate us amusing ourselves at her expense, but then she laughed, too, and all the tightness in her body disappeared. "I want to see everything, try everything, do everything," she said.

We tried to do it all. We rode the flying horses. We threw balls at milk bottles. Jesse should have won a tiny china dog when her last ball hit the top shelf. All the fancy prizes on it tumbled down, knocking over the milk bottles faster than any baseball could have. The man in charge grumbled, "It don't count if it ain't the ball that knocks 'em over," and sent us on our way. We paid a penny to the man who guesses ages and weight, and Jesse collected a dime when he guessed that Jesse had to be at least eighteen. We even visited one of the gypsies. Daniel was the only one brave enough to have his fortune told. But I couldn't let him go in alone, so Jesse and I followed him into the tent and stood behind him while the gypsy studied his palm.

"You will have four fine sons and a long life," she told him. Then she frowned. "But I see shadows here. A loss. Much grief."

"I lost my black spotted snake in the back fields the other day. Caused me no end of grief," Daniel joked.

The gypsy was not amused. "Do not hold the Fates in light regard, young mister. Shadows do not lie. The dreams you wish will not come true, and your sadness will be with you all the days of your life."

Her words made me shiver inside that hot tent, but once we were in the light of day again, the gypsy and her prediction seemed silly. "I don't know how she could see a shadow on your hand when the whole tent was dark," I said.

Daniel grinned. "Little sister, I can see into the future just as well as that old gypsy woman. Here's my prediction for you: Never in your life will you be deceived by some con man."

Jesse wasn't listening to us. "What haven't we done yet?" she wanted to know.

Daniel and I answered together. "The Ferris wheel."

He loved the Ferris wheel. I didn't. It was one of those things I had never quite dared to try. A hundred times my father, my mother, and Daniel had told me they would ride it with me. They even promised not to jiggle the seat. But a hundred times I had refused, although I longed to see the world from so high up. I'd get right up to the man collecting tokens, then I'd lose my nerve. Once I went so far as to actually sit in the seat, but at the last second I started hollering to get down. My father had to give the man running the wheel a dime to let me off.

"You go on. I'll wait for you here," I said.

"Are you afraid? Is that it?" Jesse asked. "If you're afraid, we'll all ride together, so you won't have to be. Just think, we'll be able to see things for miles around—fields and hills and the whole town. I bet we'll even see your house and Hannah's, too."

"I can't. It's just something I can't do," I said miserably. It was like so many other things I was too afraid to try.

"Then I won't go on either," Jesse declared.

But that wasn't fair. She wanted to ride that Ferris wheel. The whole time we were talking, she couldn't keep her eyes off it.

Daniel just waited. He didn't remind me of my past cowardice, and a bubble of gratitude welled up in my heart. I knew this ride would give him a chance to finally be alone with Jesse. If I could convince her to go, that is. "You go ahead, Jesse. Please. Daniel will go with you. Then you can tell me all the things you see. You know how boys are. They can't describe worth spit. I'll feel like I was right up there with you if you go. Please!"

Jesse hesitated. "If you really don't mind, Charlie . . ."

I knew she'd be inspecting my face for any sign of upset, so I made sure I wore a smile. "I'll wait right here until you get back," I told her.

It killed me, though, seeing them go off like that. I felt left out, the way I'd felt my whole life. As I watched them stand in line, Jesse actually smiled at something Daniel said, though the smile was so fleeting he probably didn't even notice it. Then they handed the carny their tokens, and Daniel placed his hand on Jesse's back to help her into the seat.

The Ferris wheel turned slowly. I could see Jesse and Daniel, close at first and then far, around and again. The way it moved reminded me of the square dancers I'd seen down at the Grange Hall. Up there, they were doing more talking than they'd ever done standing on earth, and all because I'd given them the chance. What a good person I must be. But the sight of them getting along so well without me made my heart drop to my feet. She'd never be just my friend again. She'd be Daniel's, too. The thought rotated around in my brain with each turn of the Ferris wheel. It made me more afraid than any jolting of the seat would have.

"Charlotte Matthews? Why, I never expected to see you here all by your onesy!" I jumped half a foot at the sound of Sara Avery's silky voice.

"Imagine it, Joanna. Charlotte, you know Joanna. Well, we were just this minute talking about your brother and how he'll be finishing up high school soon."

Joanna Avery stood behind her sister. I didn't dislike Joanna the way I disliked Sara. She didn't have Sara's sneaky ways or her cruel mouth. But one look at Joanna and I figured Daniel would forget all about Jesse with her hand-me-down dress and short curls. Poor Jesse couldn't hold a candle to Joanna, who stood there smiling prettily in her yellow sprigged shirtwaist with its white lace trim and satin bow.

"Nice to see you again, Charlotte," Joanna said.

"Yes, you too. Thank you."

It killed me to say it, but Ma's lessons on manners were hard to forget. "Happy birthday, Sara," I told her.

She didn't even answer. She was too busy pretending to be concerned. "So you are truly here all by yourself?"

It wasn't any of her business. She shouldn't have had any hold on me any more. But somehow she still did, because instead of ignoring her, I pointed up to the Ferris wheel and the seat carrying Jesse and Daniel.

"I see. That's nice of your brother. Bein' kind to an orphan girl like that. I'm sure Jesse appreciates it. Seems like she's found a place in your family. First she's friends with you . . ." She paused. "And now she's friendly with your brother."

I knew exactly what she was implying—that Jesse had become my friend just so she could be near Daniel. Sara Avery was an evil, nasty thing, and I wanted to slap her face. But I didn't. I just stood there, trying not to listen to her sly comments on Jesse's character.

Finally, the torture ended. The Ferris wheel sputtered to a stop, and Jesse and Daniel got off.

In my life, I never saw a body look quite so green as Jesse.

"Jesse, are you all right?" I rushed to her side.

Daniel was steering her toward a spot behind one of the booths. Joanna spoke up, hopefully. "Daniel?"

"Haven't time now, Joanna," he said. He scarcely

looked our way as he hurried Jesse along.

Joanna choked down whatever she'd been planning to say, as if she'd prepared an entire speech but got shoved off the stage at the last moment. She cleared her throat a few times, then tried speaking again. But this time she was talking to me.

"We—Sara and I—were hoping that you—all of you—would walk around the carnival with us." She said it real politely, gracious about including Jesse and me in her invitation. I couldn't help respecting her manners.

Sara's face looked about as dark as a thundercloud. She started to walk away in a huff. Then Daniel called to me from behind the booth. "We need some water or ice, Sissy!"

My feet had already started moving when I remembered my own manners. "Maybe some other time, Joanna. But thank you just the same," I told her, waving as I hurried off.

I made a beeline for the beverage booth and came back as quickly as I could. All I'd been able to find was lemonade.

The Avery girls were nowhere in sight, which was a good thing, because Jesse was sick as a dog. Daniel held her shoulders while she threw up all over his shoes. Then he sat her on a crate and wiped her mouth with his clean handkerchief. "It's all right," he said, like he was soothing one of his wild creatures. I handed him the lemonade and he forced her to drink it, parting her lips with the lip of the glass.

We stayed there, not saying anything, until Jesse finished most of the lemonade.

"I'm sorry," she whispered in a little girl's voice.

"I got sick on the flying horses the first time I went on them," I told her.

"It was so beautiful up there," she said. "It was like being a bird. But then . . ."

"You still look a mite green around the gills, Jesse," Daniel said.

We watched my brother clean his boots with the handkerchief. Then he stomped his feet in the dirt. "I'd better be getting home," Jesse said. The tiniest smile touched her mouth. "You two should have gone off with those girls. Would have been a bit less of a spectacle."

"Can't imagine a place I'd rather be than right here cleaning spit off my shoes. Right, Sissy?" Daniel joked. He said it with such affection that nobody could have taken offense at his teasing. "You two stay here for a minute — or maybe it's best you move on a bit. Give someone else a chance to get sick. I'm going to get some more lemonade."

"I can't swallow any more," Jesse said.

"I didn't say it was for you, did I? I'm feelin' a bit on the green side myself. How about you, Sissy?"

He walked out around the booth. Jesse watched him leave. Her eyes might have been old this morning, even just a few minutes ago, but right now they were bright and shining like new. The way they sparkled, you'd think she had won every china dog and every dime in the whole carnival. But all that happiness came from Daniel, not me, and right then I felt nothing but jealous.

The Runaway

The weather must have been paying heed to my unhappiness, because the sky clouded up just as Daniel returned with two glasses of lemonade. It gave me an excuse to say, "It's probably time we start gettin' on home. It looks like it's gonna rain buckets."

Daniel must've thought I was pushing to leave so's Jesse could enjoy her party before she hurried home to Hannah's. "You might be right," he said. "Don't want to be caught here in a downpour." He started to help Jesse stand up, but she brushed his hands away.

"You don't have to fuss over me. I'm not some sick old lady." I had to admire the way she could hide her true feelings. From the sharpness in her voice, you'd have thought she could barely tolerate the sight of Daniel. It made me feel kind of sorry for him. He'd been real gentlemanly about her getting sick all over his boots, and I hated to see him getting his feelings trampled on like that. But I couldn't help being glad that he and Jesse wouldn't be making cow's eyes at each other any time soon. Daniel didn't seem to notice her rudeness. He gulped the rest of his lemonade and mine. Then he said, "Shouldn't we be heading on towards home?"

We followed him off the grounds, pausing while he returned our glasses to the lemonade booth. Jesse and I could easily have walked on ahead, but she wanted to retie her boot. "It's a bit tight after all this walking. We might as well wait for your brother at the same time. It's only polite."

"Oh, Jesse," I wanted to say. "You can fool Daniel, but you can't fool me. All this pretending doesn't hide the fact that you have feelings for my brother."

She kept up the pretending. Just like before, we walked side by side, leaving Daniel whichever part of the road he wanted. And just like before, he kept up an endless stream of chatter.

"Hannah will be glad to see you home so early," Daniel said as we passed Hastings Feed and Grain on the way back to town.

Jesse was noncommittal. "I suppose."

"'Course you could always stop by our house on the way home. Ma'd be glad to see you. She's always talkin' about how you hardly come around any more."

Hardly come around? There hadn't been a day this past week that Jesse hadn't paid a call.

"Your mother's real nice," Jesse said. "But I'd like to be home before it rains."

Daniel shaded his eyes and peered up at the sky. "I don't think there's any cause to worry. The way I see it now, the rain should hold off until after supper. Besides," he added, "you could visit Max. He hasn't seen you today, and I bet he's doin' a lot of complainin' about that." Daniel was smart about a lot of things. I had to give him that.

Jesse would have trudged through the century's worst blizzard to see her kitten.

His plan worked. Jesse doubled her walking speed. "We should be getting on then," she said.

We were at our house quicker than a fox could catch a chicken in a henhouse. The spicy aroma of Ma's best gingersnaps reached us as soon as we turned into the walkway.

"Let's go in the front door for a change. It'll give Ma a surprise she won't soon forget," Daniel suggested. I agreed immediately. Jesse was suspicious. She looked back and forth at each of us. Her eyebrows formed question marks on her forehead, but she followed us up the front steps, past the white wicker furniture Ma kept for company, and waited while Daniel knocked politely on our own front door.

Ma greeted us like she was greeting royalty. All dressed up in her Sunday best, she wore a tucked white shirtwaist and her prettiest summer skirt, a mint green serge with emerald satin trim. Covering both was her fanciest apron, all cut work and crocheted lace.

"Come right in," she said, sweeping us into the hallway.

Flowers from our garden filled the big cut-glass vases Grandma had left us when she went to the Hereafter. The vases decorated the polished maple table that was usually cluttered with newspapers and recipes my mother cut out from the *Gazette*. Ma brought us into the parlor and motioned for us to sit. Then she scooted out towards the kitchen. "I'll be back," she said. "Would you please entertain our company while I'm gone?"

Jesse didn't know what to make of it all. She sat at the edge of Ma's rose-covered wing chair, her hands folded primly in her lap. Every once in a while her head would turn toward the kitchen, looking for Ma.

"I figure this is as fancy as anything Sara Avery could concoct," Daniel commented.

Finally she understood. "You've been planning this," she said. "The carnival and everything. Getting home early."

"Actually, your getting sick the way you did was purely beneficial," Daniel said.

"Who got sick?" Ma asked as she carried a tray into the room and placed it on the table under the front windows.

Ma had done herself proud. The tray was so full I couldn't imagine how she managed to carry it. Grandma's crystal pitcher held iced tea with curls of lemon floating on top. She poured the cool liquid into each of the four matching glasses before handing them to us. Along with the gingersnaps, the same kind of fancy petit fours that Ma had made for my graduation sat on our best serving plate. Tiny cupcakes, frosted in pastel shades of blue and pink and peach and yellow, surrounded the plate, looking like petals on some exotic flower.

"Who got sick?" Ma repeated.

I didn't hear Daniel's answer. I was too busy watching Jesse's face. The "old" look was back in her eyes again, but it was fighting mighty hard with something else I had never seen there. Tears. She managed to hold them back with a struggle, and her voice barely trembled when she finally spoke.

"This is really fine, Mrs. Matthews."

"Wasn't just me," Ma said. "It was Daniel and Sissy, too. Their idea. It's your special day, you know."

"You didn't need to do this just because of Sara's party. I've missed a lot of parties in my life, and I expect I'll miss a whole lot more before I'm old." She sounded almost angry, and I looked at Daniel, puzzled.

He always understood people's feelings better than I did. "This has nothing to do with Sara's party," he said. "We concocted this for a different reason altogether—Max. Today is the day you take Max home. Today the kitten from Hades goes home with you, so he can torture you instead of me every morning."

Daniel and I attacked the food like it was our last meal on earth. But as much as Ma coaxed, Jesse barely ate. She sampled a cupcake, nibbled the edge of a cookie, and licked a bit of icing off one of the petit fours. At first, I thought maybe her stomach upset had come back. Finally I decided her lack of appetite was because of Max. Jesse wasn't sick. She was just too excited to eat.

Ma must have decided the same thing, because about ten minutes after we started digging into her feast, she said, "I think it's about time to bring out the guest of honor, don't you? Daniel, why don't you track him down? He should be hunkered down in the pantry somewhere. I gave him some milk to keep him occupied, but by now he's probably knocked over half my jars of preserves."

Jesse didn't move a muscle until Daniel returned with a squirming, complaining Max in his arms. The kitten wore one of my hair ribbons, somewhat the worse for wear because he'd chewed on it and left tiny pinprick holes in the

107

bow. My brother handed him to Jesse, and he squirmed some more while she buried her nose in his fur. Her voice was muffled. "I don't know how to thank you."

"Thank us by taking this creature from the netherworld home with you," Daniel teased.

"He's a kitten. Kittens are supposed to be mischievous." Jesse let Max crawl up her arms and across her shoulders. She plucked his tiny claws from her dress and settled him on her lap. He immediately escaped to the table where Ma's treats lay and sampled them before she had a chance to scoot him away. We couldn't help laughing at his boldness.

Ma leaned over and removed the hair ribbon from his neck. She stroked Max's fur as she did so. She'd miss him, just like she'd miss Jesse's visits. "Nothing like a kitten in the house to make you feel young," she said.

"Then Hannah will feel like she's twenty again," Daniel said. "'Course, that's if she remembers what twenty feels like."

Jesse didn't say anything. She was too busy adoring Max.

The party didn't last long after Max made his appearance. Jesse seemed anxious to get him home. She was as restless as her kitten, wiggling this way and that on the edge of the chair. Daniel found a basket in the kitchen and lined it with a square of Ma's best silk. Then Jesse placed Max inside.

"That should hold him most of the way," Daniel said.

"Yes. It will. Thank you." She wouldn't look at Daniel—or me, either—but she turned before she walked through the front door. In a quieter voice than usual, she said, "Thank you all very much. We'll come visit you soon, both of us. I really do appreciate all this. This is the best party I've been to in a very long time — maybe ever." Then she hurried out the door and down the porch stairs.

Ma curled the discarded ribbon around her hand, placing it on the tray. "Well, that's that," she said.

Daniel was nearly right about the rain. It held off until after my father came home. Then it started, a sprinkle at first, soon a steady patter. By the time supper was over, it had become a deluge that beat against the stoop with droplets that bounced once or twice before they decided where to land.

Pa was reading in his rocking chair, and Ma sat on the sofa next to him, finishing her newest embroidery donation for our Independence Day fair. Daniel sat at the pianoforte, picking through sheets of music, playing a chord from one song and a line from another. His plunking away drove me to distraction. I retreated to the kitchen and sat at the table with *Wuthering Heights* propped open in front of me, but I couldn't read a word. Too many images tumbled through my brain. Daniel and Jesse on the Ferris wheel. Jesse's sparkling eyes. Jesse's face when she tasted "Fairy Floss."

A soft tapping interrupted my thoughts. For a moment, it sounded like rain blown against the back door, but then it stopped. A minute later the tapping came again, this time accompanied by a muffled voice.

I slid off my chair and opened the door wide. Jesse stood on the stoop, soaked to the skin.

"Jesse, what are you doing here? You'll catch your death of cold. Come in here out of the rain."

She took two steps inside, closing the door behind her. "I just wanted you to know, seeing as how you're my friend, and seeing all your family's done for me, that I'm leaving," she whispered.

"Jesse. No!"

"I'm not leaving Turner's Crossing. I'm leaving Hannah's house. So if you go looking for me there tomorrow, you won't find me."

"It's pouring out! Nothing's so bad that you can't at least stay the night there."

"She threw Max out—just threw him out the door into the rain, like he was a bug or a rag or a piece of dirt under her feet. I can't stay with someone that hateful." Her voice shook with anger.

"She didn't know you'd be bringin' him home?"

"I told her—all the time—about how I was going over to your house to feed him and make sure he was well. Maybe I didn't tell her I'd be bringing him home in so many words. I thought I did. But the minute she saw him, she said, 'I don't want none of those filthy, sneaky critters in my nice clean house,' and threw him out. As if she'd ever dusted a shelf before I came along! It took me forever to find him again. He was all huddled up under the porch, wet and covered with mud. Max never did a thing to her!"

"So you'll keep him here, Jesse. You don't have to leave Hannah's. Ma won't mind. Neither will Pa. You can visit him just like before. He'll still be yours. We'll all understand that. And you'll be able to stay at Hannah's."

"I can't do that, Charlie. I can't go back to that house knowing what a hard, unfeeling woman she is, throwing out a helpless little animal. Max must have been so afraid, waiting for me, thinking I'd abandoned him. Besides . . ." Her voice cracked slightly. I couldn't tell if it was the rain or her own tears that dripped down her cheeks. "He's mine. I'm responsible for him, and I'm not about to give him to someone else. People always do that, and I don't want to be one of those people. I know he's only an animal, but he's mine. I'm the one who has to take care of him."

I should have known better. Jesse would never abandon any creature the way her father had abandoned her. I waited a long time before asking the next question.

"Where will you go?" Somehow I knew what she was going to say before she said it.

"Mr. and Mrs. Phelps will take me in. He said so that day in his store. He even likes cats. He said that, too."

"No! Jesse! You can't stay with Aaron Phelps. You stay with us. I know my parents will give you a place. I know they'd take you in a heartbeat."

"I can't do that, Charlie. You know I can't."

"Why not? You like it here. My mother likes you, and so does my father, and Daniel . . ."

"I don't think it would be a good idea." She hesitated. "Daniel's already too fond of me."

"So? You're fond of him, too. That's not a bad thing."

"It'd just make for problems. Believe me. I know about such things. And I won't be a cause of trouble in your house."

I grasped for anything. "What about the Grahams?

111

The sheriff and his wife? They'd take you in, at least until we can work something out."

"They got their own baby now. Their own lives. The Phelpses wanted me all along. I just got sidetracked is all."

"At least stay here tonight. Ma will talk to Hannah in the morning." Ma could convince anyone to do anything. I knew that from experience.

Jesse's voice hardened. "I'll be leaving now, Charlie. I just came to let you know where I'd be."

I couldn't stop my own tears. "You can't go. I'll never see you! You know how my parents are about Mr. Phelps. They hardly ever let me visit the store."

"Then I'll come here," she said lightly.

Something wiggled under her shirt. "I've got to go now. Max here is getting restless. And all my clothes are soaked." She pointed to a stuffed pillowcase resting against her leg. "I'll see you soon," she said.

She reached out and hugged me with one arm. "Don't worry, Charlie. I told you I can take care of myself." And she was gone.

I took a moment or two to try to control my face. Then I walked into the living room.

I mustn't have hidden my upset very well, because Pa nearly jumped out of the chair when he saw my face. "What's the matter, Charlotte?" he asked right away.

"Hannah threw Max out into the rain, so Jesse ran away. She's gone to stay with Mr. and Mrs. Phelps."

Ma bristled right up. "Henry, you go after that girl and bring her back here," she said to my father.

"It's no use, Ma," I told her. "She won't go back to

Hannah's, no matter what. She says she can't live with someone who's so hateful. She doesn't want to put us out, either. She's going to stay with the Phelpses. Mr. Phelps offered to take her in any time."

My mother was upset. "Go after her, Henry. We can't let her go off on her own, and the last person she needs is Aaron Phelps."

But my father stayed in his chair. "The girl's got a mind of her own, Liza. We can't change it for her. Sissy, if you tell me it'll do some good, I'll drag her back here by the hair, kicking and screaming if need be."

But I couldn't tell him that. Not even with Daniel's eyes boring into mine, willing me to give the go-ahead. I knew Jesse was even more stubborn than Ma. I shook my head.

That was enough for Daniel. "I'll go after her myself!" he said. He was halfway through the parlor door before Ma stopped him.

"No, Daniel. Your father's right. Jesse's not a child. She's got a mind of her own." Her voice broke a little, and she turned to Pa. "But to live with Aaron Phelps and his wife? Isn't there something you can do, Henry?"

"Not tonight. Maybe not at all, since Doc Kennett approved their application. You can't use the law to exclude a person just because you can't stand the sight of his face. Tonight Jesse'll have a roof over her head and a place out of the rain. She'll have her kitten, too. We'll see about tomorrow." He spoke in his best lawyerly voice, but he looked as unhappy as Ma. Daniel, I knew, was way past unhappy. He had stormed out of the parlor and up the stairs.

The Bargain

During all the years I sat in school listening to Sara and her friends giggle to themselves about this or that, I never felt quite so lonesome as I did after Jesse moved in with Mr. and Mrs. Phelps. She was staying there, all right. We knew because Pa checked on her for us. He'd even talked to her the very next morning. "She says she's just fine, thank you very much, and to tell everyone that Max is fine, too, and that she'll drop by to see us sometime soon." He'd stopped home at lunchtime just to tell us, but he said it all in a too-cheerful voice, if you asked me.

"Was Aaron Phelps standing there whilst you were talkin'?" Ma asked.

"He showed his face a couple of times. One time just to tell me to mind my own business." He said this lightly, like it didn't matter, but later that night when he thought Daniel and I were safely asleep, he told Ma what he really thought. Just like when I was younger and curious about what adults said in the middle of the night, I sat on the top landing and listened to my parents' conversation.

"The man's got his skin on backwards," Pa told my

mother. "I just hope Jesse doesn't get on the wrong side of him. I asked him if he minded if Daniel and Charlotte visited, just to say hello. He bristled right up like a pine cone. I think they'd best stay away for a while. Don't want him to take out his temper on Jesse. I've got a feeling the man's quite capable of that. I'm feeling kind of badly about lettin' that girl run away from Hannah."

"No, Henry. You were right. There's nothin' you could have done. She made her own decision."

"That doesn't ease my mind much, darlin'."

I didn't relay this information to Daniel. I didn't have to. He was standing behind me when I turned to go back to bed. His flushed face and clenched fists told me he had heard as much as I did.

"She should have come here instead. You or Ma could have convinced her. Pa's right. We should never have let her stay with the Phelpses," he hissed.

"Once Jesse makes up her mind, there's no changing it," I said.

But his words bothered me all night and every waking moment for the next few days. A thousand times, I recalled every syllable I uttered the night Jesse left Hannah's, and a thousand times I rewrote the ending where she walked off into the rain. Maybe I hadn't done enough. Maybe there was just the right word I could have said to change her mind. Maybe my jealousy about her and Daniel had shaded the things I did say.

Ma misunderstood my silence. "You must be missing Jesse something awful," she said.

My eyes filled right up. I did miss Jesse something awful, but that wasn't what was buttoning my mouth shut. It was more like guilt, like feeling responsible for something bad.

She patted my hand. "Don't worry. Once she settles in, she'll come around. Who knows? Tomorrow, maybe. Maybe even today."

Ma was wrong about that, too. As the days passed, though, she became more right about me hushing up because I missed my friend. There was no more Jesse knocking on our back door early every morning, no more sharing dreams with her on the back stoop, no more teaching her to count cricket chirps in the evening to find out what the temperature would be the next day. I felt lost, as if she had died, because it seemed our friendship had. Except for reports from Pa, who spotted her through Phelpses' window sweeping or waiting on customers, she might as well have dropped off the face of the earth.

Daniel pouted. In my whole life, I could never remember my brother spending more than ten minutes without a smile on his face. But with Jesse gone, he acted like he was attending a never-ending funeral.

Most days, he disappeared into the barn right after breakfast and didn't come back until supper. But every time, before he went off, he asked my mother, "Why don't we call and see if Jesse can come by for supper?"

She always gave the same answer. "You got to give the girl some time to get herself settled, Daniel."

The Monday after Jesse ran away, he repeated his question. This time Ma must have decided that enough time had gone by. Either that or she couldn't stand us moping around any more. "That's a fine idea," she told him. "I'll talk with the missus and see. She's a mite more amenable than Mr. Phelps."

She lifted the receiver off the wall and cranked the box a couple of times. "I'm tryin' to get through to Amanda Phelps," she said to Sally Bunnell, the operator. Ma's face wrinkled up when she finally got through and laid out the invitation. She nodded a few times and said, "Yes, I see." Her cheeks turned red. "Yes, I see," she said again. Then she slammed the receiver down without saying good-bye.

Her imitation of Mrs. Phelps's mousy voice was dead on. "I don't know. The girl's been helpin' my husband with the store. I'd have to check with him first. He's a mighty busy man, you know. Keepin' people in this town clothed and fed isn't a nine-to-five job. And the girl's got to earn her keep."

Daniel didn't wait to hear the rest of what Mrs. Phelps had to say. He strode out of the kitchen, slamming the door behind him.

I found him in the barn, currying Jake as if he was getting him ready for the county fair in Jamesport.

"It's like they're keepin' her prisoner," he complained when he saw me. This was the first time he'd said more than two words to me since Jesse left Hannah's.

"You can stop blamin' me, Daniel. I didn't throw Max out, and I didn't let Jesse walk away from Hannah's, either. I tried to stop her." Saying the words like that, so mad and confident-like, I actually started believing they were true. "There's nothing anyone could have said that night to change her mind. I've thought about it and thought about it. Jesse's been takin' care of herself almost her whole life. She knows what she wants and doesn't want."

He nodded. "I know. It's just that . . ."

"You wanted to take care of her yourself."

For the longest time he just stood there, the brush in his hand poised over the mule's glistening back. Then, slowly, he placed it on the shelf at the back of Jake's stall. A smile broke out all over his face. "You know something, Sissy? I got a hankerin' for some lemon drops. And maybe a couple of peppermint sticks. You bein' such a good sister and all, how's about if I treat you to some, too?"

We told Ma we were going to see the carnival fold itself into the small wagons it traveled in. She looked us up and down twice. I don't think she believed a word we said, but she didn't stop us.

We marched ourselves right over to Phelps Drug and Emporium.

Mrs. Phelps was no place around. Neither was Mr. Phelps, or at least we didn't see him. Jesse was by the door, sweeping the floor and raising enough dust to hide a man in the cloud that resulted. She looked up when we walked in, then looked down again, her head buried in her chin. She didn't bother to say hello.

That didn't stop me. I walked right up to her. "Hello, Jesse."

It was like she made a decision or something. One second her head was tucked into her chest, and the next her shoulders stiffened and her head came up, proud as you please. A shiner the size of Ohio took up the left side of her face.

Daniel, standing behind me, caught his breath. "Jesse!"

Mr. Phelps was there, all right. He'd been behind the counter the whole time, bent over the lower shelves. He straightened up when he heard Daniel's voice. "You there, boy. You lookin' for anything special?"

Daniel ignored him. "How did that happen, Jesse?"

She shook her head.

"You bump into something? Hit your face against a wall? Or did someone hit you?"

Mr. Phelps walked over to her and placed his big hand on her shoulder. "You got a problem here?"

Daniel spat his words out. "I'm not talkin' to you, Mr. Phelps. I'm talkin' to Jesse. I asked her how come she looks like she's been beaten. Maybe you got some thoughts on that, Mr. Phelps?"

I felt a chill creep right up my back and spread to my fingers and toes. No fear I had ever felt before was like this. "Please God, please God . . ." I prayed silently, without knowing what I was praying for.

"You better get out of my store and tend to your own affairs, boy. Don't be bothering my girl here." He slung his arm around Jesse's shoulder and patted her behind like Pa sometimes did to Ma. Jesse didn't even flinch.

"We're not leavin' without her," Daniel insisted.

"Jesse, come with us. My parents will take you in. I know they will," I pleaded.

"It's all right," Jesse said dully. "Everything's all right here. You best be going home where you belong. This is where I belong."

"No!" My voice cracked. "Oh, Jesse."

"You're not staying here," Daniel said quietly. He grabbed her arm, but she pulled away.

For the first time, there was some spark in her. "You can't tell me where I can or can't stay, Daniel Matthews. Go home. I didn't ask you to come here, and I don't need your help." Her tone was gentler when she addressed me. "You go home, too, Charlie. Like I said, this is where I belong."

Daniel stood for a moment, staring into Jesse's defiant face. Then his whole body deflated. Without another word, he turned and walked towards the door.

"You tell that father of yours I don't want any of his brats settin' foot inside my store and botherin' my help," Mr. Phelps called after Daniel. He hissed under his breath as Mrs. McMartin entered the store. "You best be gone before I get back, too, girlie," he said, glaring directly at me. He put on a big phony smile, like he was lord over all, and walked off to lend the woman a hand as she pushed through some boxes lying in front of the bird feeders. "Miz McMartin," he called, "I got just the thing you're needin' for those feathered friends of yours."

"Oh, Jesse," I said again. I couldn't think of anything else to say.

"I made a bargain, and I'm keepin' it." She might as well have stamped her foot.

"How's Max?"

She smiled, then winced, like her whole face hurt, just like it hurt me to look at her. "Max sleeps on my pillow and wakes me with a pat on the cheek every morning."

You could see how much she loved that kitten.

"Come home with me, Jesse," I said. "Bring Max."

She shook her head. "I can't do that, Charlie. I made a bargain."

"But he's so cruel."

She looked away. "I made a bargain. I know you don't understand and you're angry with me. I'm sorry."

"I'm not mad at you, Jesse."

"Yes you are, Charlie. You think everything is simple, like it is for you. But nothing's that simple for me. I have to go now. I have to finish sweeping out the store."

"Good-bye, Jesse."

"Tell Daniel . . . tell him I'm sorry."

We just stood there facing each other. Aaron Phelps had bruised more than her face, I thought. Her eyes no longer looked as old as Methuselah's—they just looked empty, like something inside her had died even though her body was still alive. I couldn't bear it any longer. "I have to go," I told her.

"Wait," Jesse said. Quickly, she scanned the store, checking on Mr. Phelps's whereabouts. Just as quickly, she grabbed a scrap of paper and a pencil from behind the counter and scribbled on it. The writing took her a while, partly because she kept looking up to see if Aaron Phelps had noticed what she was doing. Luckily, he was too busy pouring his charm on Mrs. McMartin to wonder about Jesse. Finally, Jesse folded the note and shoved it inside my pocket. "Don't tell," she whispered.

Daniel had waited for me across the street. I could tell he'd been hatching some plan by the way his shoulders had perked back up.

"You ready to go home?" he asked.

"I suppose."

"You go on ahead then. I'm gonna stop in to see Pa and find out what he can do. Jesse's just too afraid to leave with Aaron Phelps standing over her every minute. But Pa knows the law. And he was on that orphan committee."

"I don't think it's that she's afraid, Daniel. Not the way you mean. I think she's proud. She did say she was sorry, though. She wanted you to know that."

His eyes clouded over. "I'm going to see Pa. There must be something we can do." I knew there'd be no convincing him otherwise. He was stubborn. Like a mule. When he got some notion in his head, he wouldn't budge for anything. Unfortunately, Jesse was like that, too.

Jesse's note just about burned a hole in my pocket while I was talking to Daniel. When he marched off towards Pa's office, I didn't bother tagging along. Instead, I shoved my hand in my pocket and clenched the note in my fist. The second he was out of sight, I whipped it out and read it as best I could.

The note was smudged and slightly damp from my sweaty grasp. It was written in Jesse's childish scrawl. It said:

Meat me elevn oclock tonite. the rainbo feild. dont worry if you cant go if your afrade. Ill undrestand.

The Secret

There was no point in lying to Ma about where Daniel and I had been. She'd know the minute Pa came home. She knew anyway by the look on my face. "What's the matter?" she asked the minute I walked through the door. "Where's Daniel?"

"He's still in town. It's about Jesse." Suddenly, I couldn't talk anymore. The tears wouldn't stay in my throat, where they'd been stuck since I first saw the bruise on Jesse's face. My whole body shook with huge, gasping sobs from the very core of my innards.

Ma pulled me into her lap. I was too big for her by far. My long bones must have poked her thighs and chest painfully, but she held me close, and after a time I began to relax against her. Cry? Why, I could have filled a couple of buckets with my tears. Ma just kept holding me, though, squeezing my shoulders. "Get it all out of your system," she told me.

I did. I cried until I couldn't breathe any more, until I had to hiccup just to catch my breath.

"Set down right here next to me, and I'll get you a glass of water," she said.

I sipped from the glass she handed me and held the water in my mouth, swallowing only when I felt another hiccup coming on. Ma's hiccup remedy never failed—not even now.

My mother waited through two glasses of water before she said, "Tell me about Jesse."

Between sips of water and an occasional sob, I told her about everything except the note—how we'd never intended to go to the carnival grounds, how we'd walked bold as brass into Phelps Drug and Emporium. I told her about Jesse's face and Daniel's anger, and how Jesse had refused to leave. "That's why Daniel went to see Pa. To see what Pa can do. Daniel thinks Jesse's too afraid to leave."

"What do you think?"

It was hard to talk without my voice giving way. I had to take huge gulps of air before I could answer. "I think Jesse means exactly what she says," I said finally. "Mr. and Mrs. Phelps took her in and said she could keep Max. She thinks she made some kind of bargain, and she won't back out of it, not even now, no matter how much Mr. Phelps beats her."

"Not even now . . . ," she said, shaking her head sadly. "I think you're right, Sissy. That girl's got a lot of pride. Maybe too much."

Every second of that afternoon seemed like it was months or even years long. I was too agitated to do anything for long. I sat on the porch and tried reading. I went out to the barn and checked on Jake. I even pulled weeds from the kitchen garden. Mostly, I longed to tell Daniel about Jesse's note. Of course, I'd promised Jesse not to say anything to anyone. But thinking about sneaking out in the middle of the night frightened me something awful. It frightened me even more, though, to think about not doing it. Daniel would know best. He always did. If only he'd come home, I could figure out some way to ask his advice without actually mentioning Jesse's note.

But Daniel didn't get back until suppertime. He slammed through the kitchen door and went right up to his room without saying a word. Pa followed him through the door. "What's for supper, Liza my love? I'm hungry as a mule hauling hay," he said.

"We've got cold chicken and potato salad waiting on you. And Parker House rolls. Got the recipe out of that fancy cookbook you gave me last Christmas."

"What about Jesse?" I asked him. I don't know why I bothered. From the way Pa avoided the subject and the way Daniel tore through the kitchen, I already knew the answer. If anything had changed, my father would have said so right away.

"She's still with the Phelpses." Pa shrugged when my mother's eyes questioned him. No doubt they'd have more to say to each other later, when I wasn't around. But tonight I wouldn't be listening from the landing. I'd be too busy lying in my bed, plotting and worrying about sneaking out of the house. Lord, Jesse had me dead to rights. I was afraid. In my whole life, I couldn't remember being out after nine o'clock at night, at least not alone. But Jesse needed me, I kept telling myself. I couldn't back out of this.

All evening, anything anyone said to me pricked my

feelings. "You'll want to clean the table now, Sissy," Ma said when supper was finished. She said the same thing every night, but this time I had to bite the inside of my cheek to keep from hollering at her. Daniel was no help. Except to do his chores and pick at his supper, he stayed in his room.

"You feel like a roll or two to keep you going until morning?" Ma asked him as he walked through the kitchen on his way to the barn. He looked dazed, like he was walking in his sleep.

"No ma'am," he answered.

"What about you, Sissy?"

"Me?" My voice squeaked.

"You want a roll or two? You barely ate enough supper to keep a bird alive. Most times, you clean your plate like it was your last meal on earth."

"Because you're always telling me about those poor children in China!" I wanted to say. "And because you're always telling me I'm too skinny by half." I had to turn away suddenly, so she wouldn't see my eyes fill with tears.

She'd been real kind and gentle this afternoon, and I appreciated that. Even now, it wasn't really what she said that was making me cry. It was all the worrying. I felt like a piece of string, stretched out so far that I might break at any moment. If there was any way on earth I could have chickened out of going to meet Jesse, I would have. But her empty eyes haunted me. As scared as I felt, I couldn't let her down. She was my best and only friend. All her life, people had let her down. I didn't want to be like them. Everyone deserves to have someone they can count on.

At ten minutes to eleven, listening to the rhythm of my parents' snoring, I crawled fully dressed out of my bed and crept down the stairs. Every footstep sounded like a thunderclap. Every creak rang in my ears as loudly as the church bell on top of First Methodist. I snuck through the dark kitchen, slid out the back door, and stepped into the night.

The comforting sound of peepers had given way to a frightening silence. With the moon near full, the path leading through the orchard was not hard to see. But apple trees have a way of hovering over a body, and their twisted shadows chased me all the way to the back field, where I waited by the stone wall. "Jesse, hurry up," I prayed silently.

In just seconds a small figure appeared, gliding across the field towards me.

My heart stopped beating. "Jesse?" I squeaked.

She spoke in a normal tone. "It's all right, Charlie. It's me. Jesse."

I didn't tell her how scared I was. "I'm so glad to see you without Mr. Aaron Phelps around."

"Mr. Phelps doesn't want me to see anyone—least of all you or Daniel."

"Why not?"

Her face was turned toward Peterson's back fields. "Your father's a big name in this town."

"What has that got to do with anything?"

She turned toward me then. Even in the moonlight, I could see that the whole side of her face was swollen.

"Oh, Jesse. Not again." I wanted to hug her, but she kept her body so rigid I felt shy about trying to comfort her.

"It doesn't hurt. Not that much."

"You have to come home with me. Now. Please, Jesse. You know my parents would be glad to have you."

Jesse wouldn't look at me. "I made a bargain with the man. He took Max and me in. I knew there'd be a price to pay when I went there." She kept shifting her feet back and forth on the wet grass. What if Mr. Phelps notices her wet shoes? I thought. He'll know she's been out somewhere.

This was crazy! All this suffering over a kitten that weighed maybe three pounds. "That's ridiculous," I said. "No one keeps a bargain with someone who hurts them. It's not right."

"Mr. Phelps can't really hurt me. Except if he told people about him and me. Believe me, Charlie, your ma wouldn't want me if she knew some of the things I've done."

"My ma wouldn't care what you done," I said, gently, trying to act like Daniel reassuring one of his wild creatures.

"Some of the things I let him do . . ." Her voice caught. I had never known her to sound so despairing, and that frightened me far more than the sight of her poor bruised face. "He'd tell. He said he would. He'd tell the whole town, and everyone would know. Daniel would know. I don't want him to know. I don't want your mother to know."

"Please, Jesse. My parents won't mind. They'd understand. Daniel would, too."

"Daniel would never understand. I let Mr. Phelps do things to me, Charlie."

I wanted to cover my ears with my hands. I wanted to run and run and never stop. "Don't tell me this, Jesse," I whispered. "I don't want to know."

But she went on talking, like she hadn't heard me. "I knew when I went to live there that he was a certain kind of man. The kind who wants girls. I've met that kind before. But I love Max so much that I didn't want to give him away—not even to you. Because he's mine. And he loves me. I never had anything that loved me so much. I was afraid Max would forget about me and love you more."

"Please don't let this be happening," I kept repeating inside my head, even while I patted Jesse on the back and made soothing sounds. "It's all right," I told her. "I understand." Not about Mr. Phelps. I'd never understand that. But about Max. I knew what it was like to be jealous of someone even if you cared about them.

Jesse pulled back. "No, Charlie. You don't understand. I need to tell you this so you'll know when I leave Turner's Crossing . . ."

"Leave? No!"

"He does bad things, Charlie—man things. He touches me in places he shouldn't. And I let him, because of Max. But I may have to give Max to you after all. For a while, anyway. Just until I figure out what to do. I would have brought him tonight, except Mr. Phelps locked him up in the back room. He said I shouldn't have talked to you and Daniel, so he's punishing me." Her fingers touched her cheek. "And then he punished me some more."

I bent over and threw up all over the nice peonies

Mrs. Munch had planted last spring. Jesse stood there watching me. Then she grasped my shoulders with trembling hands.

"You shouldn't come by the store again," she said quietly.

I nodded, unable to look at her.

"You won't tell anyone what I just told you, will you?"

I shook my head.

"Swear it, like you were swearing on a Bible."

"I swear," I said. My heart pounded so loud I was sure Jesse could hear it.

"I'll bring Max to you some night. Some night soon. You'll take care of him for me, won't you? Just until I can find a place for us?"

Somehow I had to control my upset. Jesse needed me to be strong. "I'll take care of him, but he'll always love you the most."

"I shouldn't have told you about Aaron Phelps, but you're my friend. I wanted you to know why I had to leave. Besides, if anything ever happened to me . . ."

Her words chilled me right to the bone. If anything ever happened.

"You'd understand why. You don't hate me, do you, Charlie?"

She was wrong about me understanding why. I didn't understand any of it. But I didn't hate her, either. I just wanted this all to be a nightmare. I wanted things to go back to the way they were a week ago, with Daniel and Jesse and me wandering through the carnival and laughing at the surprised look on Jesse's face when she tasted spun sugar for the first time.

"You'll always be my friend," I told her. "Nothing else matters. You don't like or hate people because of what they do. You like them because of who they are."

Jesse struggled with tears again. But she wouldn't let me touch her. "I have to get back before I'm missed. Don't forget. I'll sneak Max to you some night."

Somehow, my face remained dry. "I'll keep him safe for you."

She started to leave, then turned one last time. "Don't tell a soul. You won't if you're truly my friend. Especially don't tell Daniel. He thinks I'm special. I don't want him to know the truth. I want one person in my whole life to think I'm special."

"I think you're special, Jesse," I said softly, but she was already gone, walking through the field, her head set firm and straight on her shoulders.

I hardly remember returning to the house or sneaking up the back staircase. But I know I never closed my eyes all night. "Oh God, oh God," I kept repeating over and over again, like an unfinished prayer. There had to be a way to help Jesse. Ma would know. Or Pa. I kept thinking that in the morning, I could explain what was going on, and why we had to get Jesse away from that horrible man. Then I'd remember that I was sworn to silence.

I hated Mr. Phelps. I found myself shredding the sheet with my fingers when I thought of what he was doing to Jesse. But mostly, desperately, I wanted to think of anything but that.

The Shot

Sometimes things happen that should be night-mares. You pinch yourself to make sure the bad-ness is merely part of some dream. But you don't wake up—you just keep wishing you could. And no matter what else you try thinking about, it all comes back to that one bad thing. That's how I spent most of the next morn-ing. Daniel told my mother he felt sick, and slept his mis-ery away. I just kept on wishing.

Until noontime. That's when Jesse knocked on our front door and I opened it. She stood there on the porch, cradling Max's limp body in the palm of her hand. His fur was slick with a wetness that I realized suddenly were Jesse's tears. She held him, just like the Bible said, "like a pearl of great price."

"I'm so sorry, Jesse," I whispered.

"It wasn't an accident," she said. "He killed him. He took Max's neck in his hands and twisted it." She didn't cry. She just looked at me with her old eyes. "I let him do what he wanted to me. He said I could have Max. He said I could keep him in the house. And I let him do whatever he wanted. Then he did this."

I wanted to stop her from talking, but I had no power left to speak. She continued in a strange, dead voice. "He said Max scratched him, so he had to be punished. But Max is just a kitten. He doesn't know any better."

"I shot him, Charlie. I shot Aaron Phelps dead while he was standing there, unbuttoning his suspenders." She took a deep breath. "I didn't shoot him for what he did to me. I shot him because of what he did to my Max. I'm going to Hell, aren't I."

Pain hit me like a fist punching my stomach, and I had to cover my mouth to keep from screaming. "Oh God, Jesse. Oh God." My body went rigid from shock. With her free hand, Jesse patted my shoulder until I stopped trembling. "It's all right, Charlie," she said.

It took me forever to get my wits about me. I kept repeating the same question over and over in my head. What are we going to do? What are we going to do? Oh God, what are we going to do?

Jesse answered my question before I could say it out loud. "I think I need to speak to your mother, Charlie."

"My mother?"

"She'll know what needs to be done."

Ma was in the garden, weeding and humming tunelessly. She looked up and smiled when she saw Jesse and me. Then the color drained from her face.

"Let's go inside," she said.

She sat with her hands resting on the kitchen table, Max's still body lying in front of her, and listened while Jesse told about shooting Mr. Phelps. Jesse stood, her hands folded in front of her like she was reciting a poem before an audience. The bruises on her cheek showed even blacker and uglier than I remembered. Ma didn't let any expression at all cross her face. Every once in a while she nodded, as calm as you please, as if she was listening to Daniel or me rattle on about our day at school. But I noticed her whitened knuckles, so I knew she was upset.

"Where is Mr. Phelps now?" she asked.

"Lying on the floor in the back storeroom."

"Jesse, where on earth did you get a gun?"

"Mr. Phelps had one. He kept it under the counter." Jesse groped inside her pocket and pulled out a silver derringer. She set it on the table in front of my mother.

Ma got up and walked to the bottom of the stairs. "Daniel! Daniel, you get your britches on and come down here this instant," she bellowed.

We heard a mad scrambling from above and Daniel soon stood in front of us, his hair sticking out in all directions, his shirttails hanging out of his pants. Jesse wouldn't look at him.

"Daniel, you hightail it down to your father's office and ask him to come home right away. Tell him I need him immediately."

Daniel's eyes flicked from Jesse to poor Max's limp body. He opened his mouth to say something, but my mother shushed him. "Now, Daniel. I don't care how sick you are. Find your father and get him here, even if you have to drag him out of court."

Daniel scooted out. Ma took one of Jesse's hands and stroked it gently. "I think we should contact the sheriff before Mrs. Phelps gets home from Jamesport, but last I heard she's not due back until after supper. Gone off visiting her mother, Sally Bunnell told me yesterday. We need to talk with Charlotte's daddy first." She spoke to Jesse as if she were speaking to a small child, and Jesse nodded. Then Ma turned to me. "Charlotte, you get me my special hatbox. The one with the wide pink band. We need something to put Max in. I don't think we should be burying him yet, not until your father says what to do. But we can make him comfortable while we're waiting." Her voice was as matter of fact as Jesse's, and I could see Jesse begin to collapse. Her face crumbled first, then her knees. Ma sat her down in a chair and knelt on the floor in front of her.

"Everything's going to be all right," Ma said, using her no-nonsense tone. Even I believed her. "Charlotte, you get movin', honey."

Pa came running in with Daniel trailing after. He didn't look at Jesse, but he listened while Ma explained that the sheriff ought to check on Mr. Phelps. Daniel whispered, "Oh, Jesse," in a voice so full of love and pain that it broke my heart. Just then I felt Pa's hand on my shoulder. I almost crumbled myself.

He leaned over Jesse's small form. "Jesse, you need to tell me what happened."

She shook her head. "He killed Max. I killed him. There's nothing more to tell."

But there was, and I knew it.

My father asked what seemed like a million questions. "When did Mr. Phelps kill Max? Where did the gun come from? Were you in the store when you shot him? Did Mr. Phelps threaten you in any way?" and so many more I lost track. Jesse answered them all in the same flat tone. "He broke Max's neck early this morning. The gun was in the drawer under the counter. We were in the back room of the store. Mr. Phelps didn't threaten to kill me, if that's what you mean." But she never said a word about Mr. Phelps preying on her the way he had.

Finally, Pa straightened up. "I'm going to get the sheriff now, Jesse. I'll bring him right back here."

"They'll hang me, won't they?" she asked in a tiny voice.

"No one's going to do any hanging. You had your reasons. The law takes that into account."

Ma was holding tightly onto my hand, but I didn't even realize it until she let go after Pa left. My brother sat next to Jesse like he didn't dare touch her. He even avoided looking at her, like he was afraid she would shatter into a million pieces if he paid her any mind. I couldn't blame him. I feared her lifeless expression and the awful silence myself. None of us spoke from the time Pa left until he returned with Sheriff Graham.

Sheriff Graham asked mostly the same questions that Pa had asked. Once, when the sheriff wanted to know when Jesse took the gun from underneath the counter, my father told her not to answer. Sheriff Graham got all discombobulated by that.

"I'm speaking as her attorney," Pa explained.

"When did that happen—you becoming her lawyer and all?"

"It just did." Pa smiled at Jesse. Then he lifted Jesse's hand and shook it. "That's if it's okay with you, Jesse."

"It's fine," she said.

"Then I'm advising you, speaking as your lawyer, not to answer that last question."

The sheriff's cheeks reddened. "Well I'm speaking as the law, and there are certain things I need to know."

They had more words when Sheriff Graham wanted to put Jesse in one of the holding cells behind his office.

"She's not going anywhere, Miles. Liza and I will vouch for her. She's not a mad killer about to strike everyone dead in their homes."

"The girl shot a prominent citizen of this town, Henry. I'm not goin' to let people think I didn't do my job. And what am I supposed to say to Mrs. Phelps when she asks what's happened to the person who murdered her husband? We'll let Judge Evans decide where Miss Irwin'll be held after tomorrow morning, but until then I'm takin' this girl down to the jail. Besides, you know there's no cause for worry. My wife will keep an eye on her."

I felt like it was all happening to someone else in another time, in a book I borrowed from the library. Their words swirled around my head like a fog that I couldn't penetrate. I didn't follow most of what they said. Too many thoughts were jumbled in my brain. Jesse in prison—maybe forever. Maybe hanged! But it wasn't right. All she had to do was tell them about Aaron Phelps. She had as good a reason to murder a man as any I could imagine. People would understand. I could tell them myself, if only I wasn't sworn to secrecy.

Daniel listened avidly. Every once in a while, when my brain cramped from too much thinking, I'd glance over at him. He might have found it hard to look at Jesse, but I'll bet he could have recited the conversation between my pa and Sheriff Graham word for word. It was like he timed his breathing for the pauses in their talking, so he wouldn't miss a syllable of what they said.

Abruptly, my father stood. "We best get this over with," he said, talking to no one in particular. Gently, he urged Jesse to her feet. "You don't have to worry. I'll be right there the whole time."

Jesse didn't look worried. She looked dead. She said one word. "Max?"

My mother hugged her. "We'll take care of him," she said.

Sheriff Graham coughed politely. "Actually, Miz Matthews, we'll have to take the body along. It's evidence, you know."

"Yes. Of course. I hadn't thought. Of course."

She handed him the fancy hatbox. He placed it under his arm, but he must have realized how ridiculous he looked carrying it, for he kept shuffling it from one arm to the other as he walked toward the kitchen door.

My father kissed Ma's cheek. "I don't know when I'll be home," he told her.

"I'll go with you," Daniel offered.

"You'll stay right here," Pa snapped. Then his voice softened. "There's nothing anyone can do right now, anyway. The best thing you can do is to stay here and help your ma with chores."

He led Jesse out of our house by the hand, and she followed along like someone's obedient little daughter. If only she had been. Remembering poor Jesse talking about her father made me sick. *Sometimes I wonder if he's tickling some other little girl's feet, kissing some other little girl good night.* If only she had been born into a family like mine. If only Hannah had been a different kind of person. If only.

All day long I couldn't stop babbling. "They have to see that Aaron Phelps was beating her. Even Mrs. Phelps has to admit that. The way her face looks. It'd give anyone reason to kill." I talked all evening long, saying the same words over and over, like I was trying to convince myself of something. "We should have made her leave the store with us the minute we saw those bruises. Then none of this would have happened. But Pa'll get her off. We can say how we saw her face, how Aaron Phelps treated her at the store. I'll bet Pa has her out on bail by tomorrow morning. You'll see. She'll be sittin' at the breakfast table, and Ma'll be fussin' over her."

Ma "uh-huhed" for a while, but she eventually wearied of listening to me. "It's probably best you be gettin' on to bed. Both of you. It's nigh onto midnight, and I'm thinkin' your pa won't be home tonight. He wants to make sure the girl's safe and sound."

Upstairs, alone with my thoughts, I was as lonesome as I've ever been. I couldn't take it for long. After pulling my nightgown over my head, I crept into Daniel's room and curled up on the end of his bed.

"She really didn't shoot him because of Max," I said.

"We all know that, Sissy. The court doesn't care about facts, anyway. All it cares about is whether something is legal or not. Mr. Phelps beatin' Jesse? That's a reason called justifiable homicide. You can't be blamed for killing someone if you're just trying to protect yourself. Jesse was afraid that Mr. Phelps would do to her what he did to her cat."

His voice had lost that pained tone. Now he sounded like a teacher explaining grammar to a class. Daniel might know a whole lot about the law, I decided, but he didn't know a blessed thing about Jesse. I would have bet my father's new boots that Jesse wasn't thinking about the bruises on her face when she shot Aaron Phelps. The man had done worse things than beating her, including killing Max.

That kitten meant everything in the world to her. Having something to love made up for all the promises people made to her and never kept. And now, because of it, she was probably going to rot in prison for the rest of her life. All of a sudden I felt old and tired of everything and everyone in the world, including Daniel. He was in the middle of explaining some point of law, but my brain gave out before his voice did. I fell asleep to the sound of his lecturing. My last waking thought was "Poor Daniel."

My first waking thought the next morning was the same one. Daniel had fallen asleep with his legs curled to one side so I'd have room on his bed. Sleeping, he looked so much younger than he did awake. He looked so much younger than I felt.

To tell or not to tell. The problem weighed my whole body down until I could hardly breathe. Telling might save Jesse's life. No one would understand killing someone over a cat. But killing a man because of his evil deeds? People understood about wickedness. As Daniel said, it was justifiable homicide. But I had promised Jesse, and telling would just be one more broken promise. This must be what it's like to be Jesse, I thought. This is why Jesse had eyes older than God's. It's what keeping secrets does to you.

The sun's light slanted through the window, and I listened carefully for voices from down below. There was only silence. That meant Pa hadn't come home yet. Gently, I eased out of the bed and pattered downstairs to the kitchen, where my mother was making bread. Her face was turned toward the doorway, and I could see tears shining on her cheeks.

"Ma?"

She didn't answer at first, although she smiled at me and shook her head.

"Are you all right?"

"I was just thinkin'," she said. "About how Max used to get all floured up in the mornings. Sometimes life seems just too sad to be lived, Sissy."

She wiped her eyes with her floury hands and blew her nose on the handkerchief she kept in her apron pocket. "For emergencies," she told me more than once.

"Pa's not home yet?"

"He stayed all night. He probably won't be home much before noon. But I'll have Daniel go down later this morning and bring him some breakfast. I packed a basket for him. For Jesse, too. In case they haven't eaten anything."

I'd go with Daniel. That'd give me a chance to see Jesse, to talk to her, to get her to tell people about the kind of man Mr. Phelps was. If I could just force myself not to be afraid. The thought of seeing Jesse, and actually having to talk to her about what had happened, made my hands shake.

Ma's hand ruffling my hair interrupted my thinking.

"You might think about rebraiding that mop of yours," she said.

"I'll do it before we go downtown," I told her.

Her hand poised over my head. "I was intending to send Daniel, not you, Sissy. I'm not sure it's proper for a thirteen-year-old girl to be hanging around the sheriff's office."

I pushed her hand away. "Ma! Jesse's hardly any older than I am, and she has to sit in that cell night and day!"

She lifted my chin so I couldn't avoid her gaze. "You were real strong yesterday, bringing Jesse to me the way you did. My pride just about bubbled right out of me. And it's real thoughtful of you, wantin' to see Jesse like this. But I'm not sure how you'll take it, seein' Jesse behind bars like that."

Strong? Me? Thoughtful? In my whole life, Ma never understood a thing about me, especially now. Here I was, feeling like a rabbit caught in a trap, and she thought of me as Joan of Arc!

"Please. I just need to see her this once."

Ma patted my cheek. "We'll see. Right now, you go wake your brother. It's high time he was up and at 'em. And don't forget to fix your hair."

No Visitors

Ma waited until Daniel was about to walk through the back door before she decided. "You better scoot along with your brother, Sissy," she said. "It'll do you good to get out into the sunshine. You need some color in those cheeks."

I wanted to grab Ma by the waist and twirl her around, like Daniel sometimes did. Now I could see Jesse and tell her I had kept her secret. That's if Daniel ever left me alone with her. He didn't plan on it, I knew. The way he strolled down the street, swinging Ma's basket of food for Jesse, he acted like he was going to a social event. I couldn't blame him, though.

Neither of us felt quite so happy after we spoke to the sheriff. "The prisoner doesn't want any visitors," he said. I thought maybe it was just Daniel she didn't want to see, but Sheriff Graham made it clear. "No visitors, no one, nohow. The girl wants to be left alone." Then he spoke a bit more gently. "You tell your ma not to worry none. My Agnes is takin' right good care of your friend. She packs quite a basket herself, you know. The girl'll explode right out of her dresses if she stays here much longer."

We walked to Pa's office and left Ma's basket with him. He gave us the same message the sheriff had. "Maybe she'll want to see you when she's feelin' a bit more like herself. It was a hard morning for her. Judge Evans won't set bail until after the inquiry, so she'll be keeping Miles Graham company for a while yet."

Daniel leaned over Pa's shoulder, inspecting the law books sprawled across Pa's desk. "Won't the evidence of her beating show that she killed Mr. Phelps in self-defense?" he asked. "The jury will have to believe us. Even Sheriff Graham can testify to the bruises on her face."

I always figured Daniel would become some kind of doctor, the way he was always fixing up animals or people. What if he turned out to be a lawyer? What if I had misunderstood him all along, the way Ma always misunderstood me? The thought made the hairs on the back of my neck stand right on end. But I figured Daniel was just interested in helping Jesse. Poor Daniel. Jesse didn't want him to see her in a jail cell, but here he was discussing how best to save her life and not caring a bit whether she had one head or two. Now that's real love, I decided. And Jesse would never know that someone felt it for her.

"What about the Wolcott case in Granby County a couple of years ago, where the wife killed her husband while he was sleeping in bed?" Daniel asked. "Didn't they let her go because he was beatin' her morning, noon, and night for years?"

Pa's smile didn't quite reach his eyes. "You got a point there, son. I intend to do some readin' up on that very subject. But you two best be gettin' on home. Tell your mother I'll be late."

Daniel explained as we headed toward home. "He's lookin' up other cases on self-defense. Ones that set a precedent, so he can cite them in court."

"Precedent?" I asked.

He didn't have a chance to answer. Hannah Akeson was sitting on her front porch, swinging back and forth in the breeze.

"You there! You Matthews children. You come right over here," she called out.

The last person I wanted to talk to was this hard-hearted old woman.

Daniel felt the same way. "We don't have time right now, Miz Akeson," he said. He stood right where he was, arms folded across his chest.

"I been hearing all this talk in town about that orphan girl of mine. You tell me, boy. Is what they're sayin' true?"

Except for a vein pulsing in his temple, you might have thought Daniel was some kind of statue. I actually had to do the talking. "If you're asking us if Jesse shot Mr. Phelps, the answer is yes."

"Jesus Lord," Hannah said. "I have lived too long, to be seein' such a thing. That little child of mine shootin' a man!"

"She had her reasons," I said.

"Girlie, I ain't sittin' in judgment. Sometimes we choose the Lord's path, sometimes not. But we all got our reasons." She reminded me of Jesse when she said that.

Hannah kept talking, to herself mostly. "Maybe I should've been more understandin'. Aaron Phelps wasn't a good man for a child like that. Seems I might have done somethin' to stop this from happening."

But Daniel was having none of her apology. "It's too late to think about what could've been different now, Miz Akeson." Without so much as a good-bye, he started walking away. I had to hurry to catch up with him.

"She could have tolerated the presence of one small cat in her house." Daniel just about spat the words out. But that's all he said until we got to our own back door. "I have to look up something in Pa's books—figure something out for him," he told me, then pushed through the door right past Ma.

"Seems to me you're forgettin' your manners some, Mr. Daniel," Ma called to him.

He had already disappeared into the living room.

I didn't have a chance to disappear. Ma latched onto one of my braids and wrapped it around her hand. "You saw Jesse?" she asked.

Telling her that Jesse wanted no part of us would have been too painful. "We weren't allowed," I said.

"Hmm," was her only response.

Ma let Daniel spend the whole afternoon reading. Meantime, she kept me busy with her chatter. She talked while I swept the kitchen, and while we folded sheets from the clothesline. She talked the whole time we were pinching squash bugs in the tomato patch.

"Sissy, I know Jesse's troubles have got your head in the clouds these days," she said finally. "I can't blame you. But we have to show this town that life goes on without Aaron Phelps."

"Yes, Ma."

"We got three tables at the fair this year, same as last year. That Mabel Peterson wanted to add a fourth, but I told her, 'I don't know how the rest of the women's auxiliary feels, but I'm on three committees already. I can't hardly breathe with all the crocheting and cooking I've been doing. I think we should leave things the way they've always been.' Mabel didn't look too happy about it."

I nodded. "That's nice," I said.

"I'll need you to help take care of things. It's liable to be busy right from the start. You know how people come from miles around just to stop by our table."

I had no idea what she was talking about. "The start of what?"

"Sissy, you and Daniel walked right by that banner hangin' in front of the school. Red, white, and blue, and letters ten inches tall. I don't know how you could've missed it. I'm talking about the Independence Day festivities—the bonfire Friday night, the fair tomorrow. You're goin' to be helpin' me. It'll keep you busy. That's the best way to get your mind off your troubles."

Spend the day at a fair? While my best friend was in jail for murder? All of a sudden my whole body felt as if it would collapse from lack of sleep.

I fled the garden and escaped to my room as soon as she pinched the last bug.

"Sissy?" Ma called up the stairs. "It's suppertime!"

Her voice startled me. I'd been dreaming about a face that was watching me from outside my bedroom window. For some reason it terrified me. I might have understood better if Aaron Phelps stared at me from the grave, but the face belonged to a little boy with dark curls and tears running down his cheeks. If I pulled the curtains across the window, I could make him disappear. I knew that, but not one of my muscles would move. I woke trembling and dripping with sweat.

My hands didn't stop shaking until I sat down at the kitchen table with Ma and Daniel. I wasn't the least bit hungry. Daniel kept his nose buried in one of Pa's law books. Once in while, he poked his head up long enough to nibble at the edge of a Parker House roll. For once, Ma didn't say a word to him about how it was impolite to read at the table. All her talk was directed at me.

"I decided not to wait supper for your father. No telling what time he'll be home."

"We saw Hannah Akeson on the way home," I said.

Daniel looked up briefly from his book. The muscles around his eyes and jaw tightened, like he disapproved of the subject.

"She have much to say?" Ma asked.

"She said she felt badly about what happened to Jesse, and that maybe she should have been more understanding. She said we all have reasons for what we do."

"Hannah's led a hard life herself," Ma said. "A lot like Jesse's, I imagine."

It surprised me, her noticing the connection between Hannah and Jesse the way I had.

"The day she took Jesse in, I thought the two of them would get along real well—after a while, anyway," she said. Then her voice choked a little. "I wish I had never given that kitten to Jesse." Ma closed her eyes for a moment, like she was trying to hold back tears. When she opened them, however, she was all business.

"This is not solving anything," she said. "Your father will do his best for Jesse. And it looks like he's got Daniel to help him, too. We got to concentrate on gettin' on with our lives. I told you this afternoon, I don't want the town makin' Aaron Phelps into something he wasn't."

From behind his book, Daniel said, "Next thing you know, they'll want to place a statue of Saint Aaron Phelps in front of the courthouse."

"That's why Sissy and I are going to that fair tomorrow. We're going to sell notions and piecework at our table like we always do."

"I don't think I can do that, Ma," I said.

"You can do anything you've got a mind to, Sissy."

"What about Daniel? He doesn't have to go?"

"He'll be busy, like you will. You forget. Daniel's been doin' your father's chores for him."

I expected to see a smug look on Daniel's face, but all I saw was misery and pain. Whatever he was looking for, he hadn't found it in Pa's books.

"Ma, you don't need me there," I protested. "Mrs. Bunnell is always pushing her way in, wanting to help."

Ma cleared the table and started washing the dishes. "That's enough, Sissy. We'll say no more about it tonight."

I didn't say any more, but my mind was made up. Ma could drag me by the hair. She could threaten me with a whipping. Whatever she did or said, I was not going to the fair the next day. How could I possibly stand to listen to the whole town crucify Jesse for what she did?

The Choice

Ma shoved her fingers into her gloves so hard that they almost poked through the other side. "Charlotte Ann Matthews, you listen to me. I won't have you hiding in the house the livelong day. You can mope just as easily while you're setting up the sewing booth. I want you dressed and downstairs in five minutes."

"A body might think you're ashamed that you ever made friends with that poor girl," she added, just before she marched out of the room and down the stairs. Her heels pounded so loudly on the wooden steps that I was sure they would leave marks.

The unfairness of Ma's words angered me into action. I did my own marching, right to my wardrobe, where I grabbed the first dress I saw. It needed ironing, and it was a bit short in the arms. Good, I thought. Let Ma be embarrassed. Let people think she didn't know how to take proper care of her daughter. After all, she didn't even know her daughter.

Downstairs, Ma never said a word about my dress. She didn't mention my hair, either, though she clucked her tongue against the roof of her mouth and reached over to pat the wisps escaping from my braids. Instead, she said, "I'm entrustin' this basket to you, Sissy. It's not that heavy—just some fancywork I've been stitching for the fair. I'll take this bigger basket. It's got some of that strawberry jam I put up near two weeks ago." Strawberry jam? The strawberries Jesse and I had picked? "Mind you, don't jostle the piecework too much. Those antimacassars are starched and ironed, and I won't get any pleasure out of havin' to start all over again."

We arrived at the school yard in time to see our neighbors drifting in with their own contributions for the fair. They jabbered with each other and wandered past the tables set up along the front walk. Ma didn't stop to pass the time of day with any of them. She chose a table near the entrance, took the basket from me, and set it down. "You sort these, whites from ivories, crochet from cutwork embroidery. The ladies like to see each one special," she said. "I'll be back after I drop off the jam."

Her leaving didn't bother me. I kept myself busy arranging her piecework—four sets of pineapple coasters, linen runners with lace edging, cutwork around the border of a dozen handkerchiefs, and I don't know how many doilies in all shapes and sizes.

Sally Bunnell came by with a hatbox full of her own fancywork. "Your mother has a fine hand for sewing," she said, admiring the runners. "I do hope she's passing that on to you, Charlotte Ann. It's a good skill to have."

"Yes, ma'am," I answered.

"Glad to see you're up and about these days. We all thought you'd be laid low, after what that orphan girl did to poor Mr. Phelps. You were right friendly with her, weren't you?"

"Yes, ma'am."

"To think something like that could happen right here in Turner's Crossing. Why, Myrtle Peterson said she's been locking her doors at night ever since. Who knows when one of those orphans might come looking for one of us!"

"Ma'am, the Grahams' little boy is only three. And they didn't place many other children round these parts."

She went right on as if I hadn't said a word. "Your father still actin' as that girl's lawyer? I suppose even guilty people need a lawyer. That's what Mr. Bunnell says whenever anyone speaks against your Pa. 'Even a murderess is entitled to representation,' he says."

"She had a good reason for what she did."

Mrs. Bunnell opened her mouth to reply, but Agnes Graham stopped by just then. Little Michael kept his hand attached to her skirt like someone had glued it there.

"Morning, ladies," she greeted us. She leaned down and whispered something in Michael's ear.

His face broke out in dimples. "Morning!" he announced.

I know what it means to cut someone dead on the spot, but I never saw it happen to a little boy before. When Michael smiled and spoke to her, Sally Bunnell just turned her back and marched right off, without even a nod.

Mrs. Graham's face was scarlet. She gathered Michael in her arms and hugged him so tight that he squeaked. Tears formed in her eyes. "That's been happening all morning," she whispered. "Townspeople. They didn't think much of Aaron Phelps alive, but now they all act like he was somebody's kind old grandfather."

I started to say something, but Mrs. Graham wasn't finished speaking her piece.

"Myrtle Peterson stopped me right in the street and said I was harboring a criminal in my home. A little boy like Michael! I told her where the dog died. Even Doc Kennett, he told me it was real easy to give somebody up. 'Before you get too attached,' he said. 'You can't be sure about these children. You can give them all the love in the world, but you can't change where they came from.' I wanted to slap his face. Someone should tell these people what kind of man Aaron Phelps really was . . ."

I had been thinking exactly the same thing. I stared at her, but she had eyes only for Michael. She smoothed his tousled hair with one hand. With the other, she held onto his shoulder as if she would never let go. He wriggled a little, this way and that, but he didn't try very hard to escape.

Pa suddenly appeared at the table, still dressed in his lawyer suit. I was never so glad to see anyone. "That's a beautiful boy you have there, Agnes," he told Mrs. Graham.

Her smile just about lit up the sky. "Thank you, Henry Matthews. That's a kinder thing than most people around here are saying."

"Don't worry your head about it," Pa said. "People always need something to get riled up about. Once the fair is over, they'll be arguing about who should've won the award for best peach preserves."

Mrs. Graham smiled again, then moved away with Michael in tow, heading towards the food table. The way people avoided being near her, you'd think she was Moses parting the waters.

"All this meanness because she and Sheriff Graham took that little boy into their house?" I asked Pa.

He shrugged. "Agnes has been kind to Jesse. Word like that gets out. People have been doin' a lot of huffing and puffing about replacing the sheriff with someone who won't mollycoddle prisoners. Like I told Miles, they'll get over it once they know the truth of the situation."

But I knew that no one would ever understand the truth except Jesse and me.

Neither of us noticed Mrs. Phelps walking in our direction. I was too busy asking why Pa was visiting the fair in the middle of the day, and he was too busy explaining that he needed to get away from the office for a while. Mrs. Phelps must have stood in front of the table for half a minute or so before we finally heard her clearing her throat.

"I have something I want to say to you," she said, staring straight at Pa. Her voice was as tiny as she was. In all my years I had never before heard her speak above a whisper.

"You have my full attention, Mrs. Phelps," Pa said.

"The sheriff says that you're that orphan girl's lawyer."

"That's true, ma'am."

Mrs. Phelps swallowed a couple of times before she spoke again. "My husband was a hard man sometimes. I'm not sayin' he wasn't. But I want you to know something. I want you there, girl, to know it too. I ain't got nothin' now, even if I sell the store and live on that money for a while. I cain't hardly take money to bed on a cold night. Aaron Phelps is the only man who ever gave me the time of day. Now he's gone. You cain't imagine what that's like."

"I'm truly sorry, Mrs. Phelps," Pa said.

Mrs. Phelps's hands trembled. For a moment I thought Pa was going to reach over to steady them. She must have thought so, too, because she stepped back.

In that same tiny voice, she said, "You remember this, Mr. Lawyer Matthews. At the bonfire Friday night, I'll be praying to God that someone throws that orphan girl into the flames. And the same goes for anyone who helps her."

Pa didn't say a word. We watched her turn and walk away. I didn't realize how much my own hands were trembling until Pa took one of them into his own and squeezed it. "It's all right, Sissy," Pa said. "She's talking out of hurt."

I had never even thought about Mrs. Phelps's suffering. Instead, I blamed her for letting her husband hurt Jesse the way he did. She saw Jesse's bruises. She should have known. But now I felt sorry for her, too. I understood that she must feel lonely and need someone to be with. What if I didn't have Pa and Ma and Daniel—and Jesse?

I closed my eyes to rest them, but it was a mistake. My mind filled with pictures. Mr. Phelps twisting Max's neck until it broke. Jesse, with that terrible blank look in her eyes, pulling the trigger. Mr. Phelps falling dead to the floor. The horror of it all filled my whole body, and I had to grab onto the edge of the table to keep from falling. Pa put his arm around my waist, steadying me.

When I opened my eyes, Ma was standing in front of the booth. "Sissy, you're lookin' green as a ghost! Are you all right?" She placed her hand on my forehead. "I saw Mrs. Phelps over here. What's going on, Henry? Why are you here?"

"I had some free time and thought I'd drop by." Pa kept his voice light, but he spoke directly to Ma. "Just making sure the world was treating you right, Liza. Lots of people are talking about things that are none of their business these days."

"People in this town always do a lot of talking," Ma said. "You can stop your worrying about us." I could tell Ma appreciated his concern, though. Her eyes had that soft look they wore whenever he reached for her hand or kissed her cheek.

Just then a woman caught my mother's arm and pulled her toward the linen runners before she had the chance to say another word.

Pa squeezed my shoulder. "Tell your ma I got a lifetime of work back at the office, so I better be gettin' on." He walked toward the gate, talking first to this person and then to that one, like nothing was bothering him. But when he left the school yard, I noticed he headed for Sheriff Graham's office instead of his own.

All afternoon, I sold handkerchiefs and coasters to women who inspected every stitch like the world revolved around straight seams and fancy crochet. I didn't pay much attention to their chatter. My mind kept going back to Mrs. Phelps—the way she was missing her husband and praying that something bad would happen to Jesse and everybody who helped her. It scared me a little.

God and I hadn't been on speaking terms in a while, but I hoped He'd listen to me anyway. Pa didn't need a whole lot of prayers on his behalf. I figured he'd shoot straight up to Heaven whether I interceded with the Lord or not. Ma and Daniel, too. But Jesse? I was deathly afraid for her, and for Michael, too.

I prayed silently. *God, please don't let anything bad happen. Jesse committed an awful sin, I know, but you understand why she did it. Please forgive her. And please don't make the Grahams send Michael back. He's just a little boy who never did wrong to anyone, and they love him so much. Reverend Sikes always says you watch over the smallest sparrow. Please watch over Michael and Jesse, too.*

In my head, I paused for a moment. *And please, God, help Mrs. Phelps stop hurting. Amen.*

Darkness shrouded my bedroom, so it must have been the stifling heat that woke me that night. My eyes blinked rapidly, trying to adjust to the blackness. "No moon," I thought. Then I heard the trickle of rain on the roof. "Clouds covering the moon," I decided. It had to be midnight or later.

My parents were still up. I could hear their voices. I crawled out of bed and slipped through my bedroom door. Down the stairs I crept until I reached the first landing. There I settled, Indian style, on the polished wood and listened to their conversation. They were talking about Jesse.

"Darlin', without any evidence, I can't hardly do a thing for that girl's defense," Pa said.

"Without any evidence? Henry, you heard what Charlotte and Daniel said about the girl's face. It was all swollen and bruised. Aaron Phelps was beating that poor child. Anyone who walked into the man's store could've seen that. You tellin' me she didn't have some cause for what she did?"

"I'm tellin' you I'm going to have a hard time convincin' a jury that this stranger, this orphan from New York City, had a good enough reason to shoot their neighbor—the man who sold them half the goods in their houses. I'm going to have a hard time persuadin' them that strangling a cat gave Jesse good enough cause to kill a man. For God's sake, half the men that'll serve on the jury have drowned a sackful of kittens or worse. And we've all whipped our children at one time or another."

"That kitten meant the world to Jesse. And it wasn't just a whippin' she got from Aaron either, not from what Charlotte says. Not from what we saw. He beat that girl."

"What Charlotte says and what I can say in court are two different things. Because her friend Jesse isn't talking. She won't say a word to me except, 'Whatever you think is best, Mr. Matthews.'"

My mother's voice sounded as scared as I'd ever heard it. "Henry, they can't possibly convict her, can they? She's just a child."

"Liza, she's fourteen. Charlie could ask the court to try her as an adult."

I was in the kitchen before I realized I had left the landing. "Jesse won't hang, will she?"

They sat at either end of the kitchen table, hands wrapped around my mother's best china coffee cups. "Come sit by me, Sissy," Ma said, pulling me into the seat beside her. She reached over and stroked my arm. "Everything will be all right." She was talking in that comforting tone, but my father's words hushed her.

"I honestly don't know what's going to happen, Charlotte," he said.

"They can't hang her, Pa. Jesse had good reasons to shoot him—and not just because of Max, either."

My father sounded tired and fed up. "Sissy, if she's got other reasons, she's not sharing them with me."

For a moment, the only sound in the house was the ticking of the clock in Pa's study.

"Aaron Phelps was an evil man. He did worse things than killing Max—worse even than beating Jesse," I said.

I watched my father transform right before my eyes. One second, he was Pa, his eyes drooping from too little sleep. In the next instant, his eyes turned to steel and his voice took on a hard edge. "What do you know about Jesse and Mr. Phelps, Charlotte?"

In my mind's eye I saw Jesse again, leaning against the Petersons' stone wall. Even in the shadows, her eyes looked older than God's. *Don't tell a soul. You won't if you're truly my friend.* She had trusted me.

"I'm sorry, Jesse," I told her silently. "Please don't hate me."

"What do you know about Jesse and Mr. Phelps?" my father repeated.

The summer I turned four, Daniel and a couple of his

friends decided I should learn how to swim. They pushed me into Joe's Pond and expected that I would paddle my way back toward the bank, where they stood waiting for me. Instead, I choked and sputtered and swallowed enough water to fill a bucket. Daniel dived into the water, grabbed me by the hair, and pulled me out. His friends ran off as he sat beside me. It was like he couldn't believe I was still alive, he hugged me so hard.

"Oh, Sissy. I'm sorry. I never thought you'd drown. Please! I'm so sorry." I forgave him right then, but I couldn't stop crying—not for hours and hours. Drowning had come too close. Now, telling my parents about Jesse and Mr. Phelps, I felt like I was drowning all over again.

I told them about meeting Jesse that night at the stone wall. About the bargain she made with that awful man. About how he touched her in ways that no man should touch a young girl. About how she was so ashamed that she couldn't tell anyone. About how Aaron Phelps threatened to reveal her sins to the whole town if she even thought about trying to run away. The whole time I was speaking, Ma's hand rested on my arm. She squeezed gently every time I hesitated, giving me courage to go on.

When I finished, my father placed his head in his hands. "Good Lord," he said. "I should have known. Someone should have known."

"Jesse will never speak to me again," I told them. "She'll hate me forever."

Ma wrapped her arms around my shoulders. "You may be right, Sissy. She may hate you. But sometimes, as hard as it is, you have to tell the truth. You may have saved that girl from spending the rest of her life in prison. She'll thank you for that—someday."

"None of what she said is true." We turned. Daniel stood in the doorway.

My mother reached for him, but he pulled away. "None of that is true!" He bolted through the kitchen and out the back door, letting it slam behind him.

"Daniel!" I started to follow him, but Ma stopped me.

"No, Sissy." Her eyes bore into my father's face. Slowly he nodded and followed Daniel out the door.

My mother motioned me to sit. She gathered the coffee cups into the sink and filled them with water. Then she sat down next to me.

"Daniel loved Jesse a lot," I told her.

"He still does."

For a time, we said nothing. Pa's clock chimed twice. "This is a nightmare after all," I thought. "Soon I'll wake up, and everything will be fine again." But I knew it wasn't true.

Ma finally spoke. "Sissy, you and me are so much alike. We want the people we love to be safe and happy. But we also know that life isn't like that. Daniel—and your father, too—they don't understand how hurtful the world is. You and me are never surprised by the pain. That makes life easier. But our lives are never quite as magical as theirs, either."

As drained as I was, I wasn't about to let Ma tell me that she and I were like two peas in a pod. "You're wrong, Ma. I'm just like Daniel and Pa. The world is magical for me, too. But you keep telling me it's not." The words surprised me, the way they popped right out of my mouth.

They surprised Ma, too. The muscles in her cheeks jumped around a little, like she was holding something back. But no anger flared in her eyes. All she said was, "Time for bed, Sissy. You don't want to get dark shadows under your eyes. Your skin is already too dark."

I leaned over and kissed her good night.

The Inquiry

I couldn't tell you if or when Daniel came up, because I don't even remember changing into my nightgown. I slept so deeply that Ma herself had to rouse me the next morning.

My first words to her were "Where's Pa?"

"He's gone to talk with Judge Evans. The county attorney, too. He wants us to meet him at the courthouse at nine o'clock." She fussed with my blanket, smoothing its wrinkles, even with me still lying there curled under its warmth. "You'll have to be moving along right quick for us to be there in time. It's already nearly eight."

"Where's Daniel?"

She shook her head. "You got to let him work things out in his own mind, Sissy. He needs to be alone to do that." That meant he was in the barn with his animals. Suddenly, lying there, I understood just what he was doing. He'd put his hands on their trembling bodies and feel their fears ease, and their trust would make him feel better for a time. That's how Jesse had felt when she held Max. His trust made her forget all the bad things that had happened to her. And that's how it had been with me and

Jesse, too. Her trust made me feel like I was someone special.

Then I remembered how I had betrayed that trust. I wanted to hide in my bed and never leave it.

But Ma wouldn't allow that. She bothered me about which dress I was going to wear. "Your Sunday going-to-meeting one seems most fittin'." She fretted about my hair, then let me wear it in braids the way I always did. Just like we were going on a picnic, she pulled a carpetbag from the closet under the stairs and filled it with cucumber sandwiches, a jar of tea with lemon, and molasses cookies. After a moment's reflection, she added her crochet hook and a ball of string. "It's liable to be a mite long waiting on the men. You might think about bringing a book to read." As if I could read. As if I could even think! My whole body was numb. Telling Jesse's secret would help her, I thought. That's what Ma said last night. But now it just seemed like I was shaming Jesse before the whole world and Daniel, too.

Ma left me alone with my worrying the whole way into town. Usually, she chattered on about this person and that one, and stopped to pass the time with neighbors. Not this morning. She nodded politely to our neighbors but told them briskly, "I'm sorry, but we've got places to be going" when they approached us.

We arrived at the courthouse a little before nine. Sheriff Graham was pacing from one side of the vestibule to the other when we arrived. "Good. You're here early. The judge is expecting us in his chambers," he said. "Why don't you wait here, Miz Matthews. I'll take Charlotte in to see the judge myself."

Ma bristled right up. "I'm not letting Harry Evans ask my daughter a thing without me being there."

"Well now, I'm not right sure about that."

"Not right sure about what, Miles?" Pa opened a door off the hallway. He kissed my mother on the cheek and squeezed my arm.

"Your wife wants to be there when your daughter says her piece."

"I don't see why Liza can't be there. If Judge Evans doesn't like it, he can say something himself."

Pa brought us through the courtroom and into a small office. My numbness disappeared. I felt like I was walking to my death, the way every little detail etched itself onto my brain: the courtroom with its smell of tobacco and lemon oil, the click of our shoes against the wood floor, the clean white railing around the jury box.

Judge Evans sat at the carved oak desk in his office. He was smoking a pipe, and he wore a white linen suit that matched his snow-white hair and whiskers. He chewed his tobacco loudly and spit into a copper spittoon that sat by the back door.

Charles Abbott, the prosecutor, sat across the desk from him. I had never liked Mr. Abbott, mostly because he and my father constantly battled each other in this very building. I could never understand how Pa could eat his lunch with a man who spoke so rudely to him in the midst of a trial, but just about every noon they walked across the street to Hamilton's for a sandwich and an ice cream soda.

They both stood politely when we came in, and Judge Evans shook my hand as gravely as he shook my mother's. "Sit down right by me, Miss Matthews," he said.

Then he sent my father to grab a couple more chairs from the jury box. "Everybody nice and comfortable?" he asked when we were all finally settled around his desk.

I sat on the edge of the chair with my eyes focused on my feet. I had never thought about Charles Abbott being there. I half expected him to jump out of his seat and poke his finger into my chest, screaming at me the whole time. "You're making the whole thing up, aren't you? Aren't you?" Pa said he had a way of turning the truth inside out and upside down.

"Now, Charlotte, your father tells me that you know something that might cast a different light on this whole unfortunate situation," the judge drawled.

My breath sputtered to a stop, but I felt my mother's hand grasp mine. I nodded.

"I'm going to ask you to tell me exactly what you told your folks last night about Aaron Phelps. You don't have to be shy or embarrassed. These walls have heard a whole lot worse than anything you've got to say. You take all the time you need."

His voice was as gentle as Daniel's when he was soothing some wild creature, and I felt my whole body relax.

"I don't know how to begin," I whispered.

He smiled at me. "Why don't you just start where it's most comfortable."

None of the telling felt comfortable, but Judge Evans was kind. I started with the note and sneaking out of the house. Every once in a while, he asked me to speak a little louder or to repeat something. Like when he asked me, "She wanted you to take care of her cat in case something happened to her?"

"Yes, sir. That's what she said."

"All right. Continue."

No one else said a word. Mr. Abbott leaned on the judge's desk and let his chin rest on his crossed arms. He listened to every word I said like he was a vulture waiting for a lamb to die, but I kept right on talking.

"So I snuck back into my room. And the next day . . ." I spread my hands out in front of me. "Jesse shot Mr. Phelps. 'I shot him dead while he was standing there unbuttoning his suspenders,' she told me."

That was it. The end. Charles Abbott opened his mouth to say something, but the judge gave him dagger's eyes. The county attorney's mouth clamped shut.

"Jesse has been your good friend, hasn't she?" Judge Evans asked.

"She's my only friend," I answered. My mother squeezed my hand.

"Your father tells me that you're a truthful young lady. That's a good thing to be, Charlotte. But sometimes people are mistaken. They don't understand when another person is pulling their leg or teasing them."

I looked straight into the man's face. "There was no mistaking what Jesse meant. Mr. Phelps was doing things to Jesse he oughtn't. And Jesse doesn't tell lies. You ask her yourself. She'll tell you, now that she knows I told."

Charles Abbott just couldn't resist asking a question. "Then why in Heaven's name didn't she say something before about all this?"

Because, you stupid man, she was more ashamed of the world knowing what she'd let that man do to her than she was of being hanged. Because she loved Daniel and

167

my mother, and she didn't want them to know. And now I had told everything before God and a judge. My eyes filled up, and I could barely answer him. "She was too ashamed."

Suddenly, in a bustle of activity, the interview was over. Judge Evans stood and shook my hand and thanked me for my honesty. The sheriff gathered the extra chairs and returned them to the jury box. My father patted me on the back and told me I had done a brave thing. To my mother, he said, "If you go wait in the vestibule, I'll be out in a little while and take you both to lunch." Ma took my hand again and led me through the office door while the men settled back into their seats. The last thing I heard as we closed the door behind us was Charles Abbott's voice. "Of course, it's all hearsay . . ."

It seemed like we waited for my father forever. I counted every block of tile on the floor at least twice. Ma spent the time crocheting a pineapple square for the tablecloth she never seemed to finish. The sheriff left once. He came back just a short time later, accompanied by Jesse. I tried to catch her eye, but she walked right by me as if I didn't exist. She was looking nowhere but in front of her.

Not long afterwards, Sheriff Graham led her out of the courtroom. But she wasn't the same Jesse who went in there with her head held up right and proud, like nothing could ever hurt her. Now her whole body drooped, and her eyes stared at the floor. The soles of her shoes scraped the tile as she walked. I wanted to say something, anything, but my words caught in my throat. There was nothing I could say. My mother reached out and grasped one

of her hands as she passed by. "Jesse, if you need anything
. . ." but Jesse shook her hand off without looking up.

"They're going to put her on trial after all," I said as
we watched her shuffle away. "I told everything. I shamed
her in front of the whole town for no reason."

Ma shook her head. "We'll just have to wait and see,
Sissy."

So we waited. Ma tore out as many stitches as she
crocheted, and every once in a while she sighed like the
whole world was leaning on her shoulders.

"They're going to put her on trial," I repeated.

I said the same thing when my father finally emerged
from the courtroom. "That's not true," he said.

"What happened?" Ma wanted to know. "They're not
sending that poor child to prison, are they?"

"No trial. No prison. Charlie agreed there were exten-
uating circumstances. Judge Evans agreed, too. She'll be
sent to Chillicothe, to the reform school there, as soon as
arrangements can be made."

"But she was protecting herself!" I couldn't believe
the unfairness of it all.

"Charlotte, she killed a man. And she'd never be able
to raise her head here in Turner's Crossing again. People
are cruel, and they'd talk about her all the time. The
school's not a punishment—not really. She'll learn a trade
and be out by the time she turns eighteen. Then she'll be
able to get on with her life."

"But it's not right!" I cried.

My father's face looked tired. "It was the best I could
do, Charlotte. What's right is not always the same as
what's possible."

My mother had her hands full. With one arm, she hugged me close. With her other hand, she smoothed my father's hair. All my life, I thought Pa was the one who smoothed things over, made life a bit gentler for us. Now I realized Ma was the one holding our family together. Pa and Daniel and me. We were all so much alike, too sensitive for breathing, torn by our set ideas of right and wrong. All of Ma's fussing and fidgeting was her way of shielding us from a world she thought was too cruel for our delicate natures. I decided that, for once, I was going to be like Ma. I'd be strong. I pulled out of my mother's grasp and looked up into my father's face.

"Thank you, Pa," I told him. "I'm glad Jesse had you for a lawyer."

"I don't think Jesse's too glad about it right now."

None of us felt like dodging questions about Jesse at Hamilton's Ice Cream Parlor, so we ate our lunch in my father's office. That's where we were when Sheriff Graham came looking for us.

"I'm glad to see you're both still in town," he said to my mother and me as he walked through the door. "That saves me a trip out to your place."

My father and me let Ma do the asking. "Miles Graham, what on earth are you talking about?"

"I'm talking about the Irwin girl. She wants to see Charlotte here. She asked especially if she could see her this afternoon."

Pa walked with me to the sheriff's office. He showed me into a back room and stood next to me while Sheriff

Graham escorted Jesse inside. The sheriff waited at the door while Jesse seated herself in the chair opposite me.

"I don't think you have any call to stay," my father said. Sheriff Graham opened his mouth as if to protest. Then he shrugged. "S'pose not," he said. "It's not really like she's a prisoner anymore. Not the way she was, anyhow." He left, closing the door behind him. Pa walked over to the window and looked out.

"You're lookin' good," I told Jesse.

Her lips pursed.

"At least as good as can be expected."

"I'm doing all right."

The silence was like death between us.

When I was a little girl, Ma always said, "Whenever you don't know what else to say, say what's on your mind." So I did.

"I'm sorry about everything. About telling and all," I said.

She shrugged. "It doesn't matter now."

"Pa says you're going away to school."

"Seems likely."

I couldn't stand it anymore. "I am sorry, truly sorry."

She looked me straight in the eyes and said, "That's not enough, Charlie. You can say you're sorry a million times over, but you still hurt me. I trusted you. You were my friend."

"I'm still your friend. I couldn't watch you hang. I couldn't stand the thought of you going to prison for something that wasn't your fault."

Her face softened. "You don't understand, do you?"

I could hardly answer for the tears choking my throat.

All I could do was shake my head. "What are you talking about? What is it I don't understand?"

Her gaze left my face and wandered over to the window where my father stood. She must have decided he was trustworthy enough, for she stiffened her shoulders and her gaze came back and held mine.

"You are so wrong about things, Charlie. You and everyone else. And I tried telling them that, but they won't listen. So I guess I'm just going to Hell after all." She paused to catch her breath. "I told you I didn't shoot Aaron Phelps for what he did to me. I didn't even care what he did to me, excepting what people might think. Your ma. Daniel. It had nothing to do with what he did. I've had worse men than him using me for their pleasure. I told you before, you learn ways to survive when your belly's empty, and I learned them all. It was his killing Max. That's what made me take up the pistol and shoot Aaron Phelps in his black heart. And I'd do it again in a heartbeat."

Her words chilled me, and I felt my knees tremble.

"So you see, I've been let out of prison for a lie. You didn't mean to lie for me, but you did. Now I've murdered a man, and I'm just gonna be free and clear in a few years without ever paying the price. I have to live with that all my life, Charlie. Knowing I killed someone, knowing I'd do it again, knowing that I won't be punished like I deserve."

The Train

When I got home, I headed straight to the barn to see Daniel. I told myself that leaving him to wonder and worry about Jesse's fate would be cruel. But it was all more complicated than that. The saying "Misery loves company" has a lot of truth in it. Truth is, I had to be near someone as miserable as I was.

Daniel had cleaned the stalls and shucked the hay and polished Jake's hooves until they gleamed like Myrtle Peterson's oak floors. He was sitting on a bale of hay, watching Lucas wash his paws in the water bucket when I opened the door.

"It's all over," I told him.

He nodded. "I figured. Ma got back a while ago. She said you'd be coming along sooner or later."

"They'll be sending Jesse away. To school. As soon as they can make arrangements."

"That's best. You always said she needed more schooling."

"Pa says it's better for her to be away from this town anyway. The way people talk."

"Turner's Crossing. Telegraph station of the world."

Daniel tried to smile, but his eyes weren't up to the task. Instead, he turned his hands over in his lap and inspected them like he'd never seen them before.

"I talked with her this afternoon," I said finally.

His head shot right up. "And?"

I sat down beside him. "Oh, Daniel." And even though I knew he loved her still, even though my heart hurt so much I thought it would burst, I told him what she'd told me that first afternoon, about how she really wasn't an orphan at all, about her father and mother and how awful life had been for her. "She just needed something to love, something that loved her back. And Aaron Phelps took that away."

Daniel turned his head towards Jake. He grabbed a handful of hay and flung it against the wall. "Why didn't she just come to us? We would have taken her in. You know how Ma is. Why didn't she come to us? Why did she have to go to a man like Aaron Phelps?" His anger erupted through the barn like a fire, and his whole body quivered from the explosion.

I touched his arm. "Because she knew you loved her, Daniel. And I think she didn't want to end up hurting you. Because she loved you, too."

We didn't say anything after that. In the corner of the barn, Xavier shifted her weight. We could hear the squeals of her piglets as they scrambled to adjust to her new position. Pa would be home soon. He'd go up to the house and stomp his dusty feet on the stoop, so Ma wouldn't lecture him about carrying all that town dirt into her nice clean kitchen. My mother'd be at the stove, getting supper ready. He'd grab her by the waist and kiss her cheek until she protested. Then she'd turn around and loosen his tie and tell him he looked too tired for words. Things like that, I thought. Things you can rely on. They make a whole lot of difference in who you are and who you become.

Daniel and I walked back up to the house together. A flood of memories filled me as we reached the back stoop: Jesse listening for Max's purr in the dark. Daniel trying to impress her with tales of school. Ma cooling her legs in the evening breeze. Jesse gave me everything. The one gift I had to give her—my loyalty—I had betrayed. All she would have to remember our friendship by was misery, grief, and shame.

Ma sat at the kitchen table, her head buried in her hands. I expected to see tears on her cheeks when she raised it, but there were none. Instead, her face was as white and pained as I'd ever seen it.

"Mrs. Graham was here while you were gone," she told us.

"She having trouble with that boy of hers? Michael?" Daniel asked.

"They're doin' just fine. It's like they were meant for each other. She thinks he's God's gift to them, just when she was losing faith. No. For the Grahams, and for Michael too, the orphan train was the best thing that ever happened to this town." She paused, and I could see her mind choosing exactly the words she wanted to say. "She wanted me to tell you something, Sissy."

"She wanted me to tell you that you were right to tell about Aaron Phelps. That other people just don't have that kind of courage. She wishes things would have worked out better. She wanted you and Jesse to know that she was sorry, real sorry. That maybe if someone had said something before, none of this would have happened."

I had a sudden memory of Agnes Graham grabbing Jesse by the arm, warning her against going with Mr. and Mrs. Phelps. I remembered how she had worked for Phelps herself when she was a girl. "Someone should tell these people what kind of man Aaron Phelps really was," she'd said at the fair.

She had no call to apologize to me or to Jesse. Unless . . .

Daniel looked puzzled. "I don't understand."

"You weren't meant to. It was a message for your sister," my mother said grimly. Our eyes met across the table, and she nodded.

Jesse left town on Thursday, July 10th. Because few people cared when Jesse would be leaving, there was no one standing at the station, watching for her train to arrive. Except me. The waiting felt long and lonesome. I wished like anything that someone was there, fidgeting alongside me. But I wouldn't ask Daniel to go, and Pa told Ma to stay away. "Jesse thinks mighty highly of you, Liza. She's pretty fragile right now, and I think she'd shatter into a million pieces if she saw you start to cry. And you know that you would the minute you saw her."

Ma sputtered a bit and muttered while she wrapped sandwiches and cookies in brown paper and tied them with string. But he was right. Jesse admired my mother so. Seeing her one last time would just about break Jesse's heart, if it weren't already lying in pieces on the Phelps Drug and Emporium floor.

Pa told me it was all right for me to show my face, though. I was kind of hoping he wouldn't. "That'd be nice, Sissy. I have a feeling she'd like to say good-bye to you," he said, and my mother ironed my shirtwaist and cuffs herself without once saying, "There's some things a young lady has to learn if'n she's ever going to live in this world, and ironing is one of them."

She would have had a conniption fit if she knew how quickly the sun ruined her efforts to make me presentable. Already it burned so hot that I could feel its warmth soak through my blouse, making it stick to my shoulder blades. Ma didn't believe in sweat. But she wasn't there to notice, and I was too nervous to care. I hadn't seen Jesse since that afternoon in the sheriff's office. I hadn't asked to. But I couldn't let her leave without me being there.

Just before nine o'clock, three figures made their way down the street toward the station. My father was one. He had left before seven, in order to talk to Jesse before she left. Ma told me he'd not rest until she was safely out of town. Not that he expected anything untoward to happen. Recently, there'd been lots of whispering about Aaron Phelps and his treatment of Jesse, spurred on by Mrs. Graham. But he wanted to make sure Jesse knew that he was watching out for her right up until she left town.

Miles Graham walked beside Pa. He'd be escorting his "prisoner" to the reform school in Chillicothe. Pa said

Agnes Graham had volunteered to go with them, but Miles told her it'd be a mite unseemly. People would say Jesse was receiving special treatment.

Then there was Jesse. She looked small and frail walking next to the two men, like a porcelain figurine. No wonder Pa thought of her as fragile. I knew better, though. Her face was set in the same mask she wore when she came to Turner's Crossing, and I don't think she saw me until she got right up to the platform.

"Jesse," I called to her.

My father, the sheriff, and Jesse all stopped. For the longest moment, I thought she'd turn her back on me. I think Pa thought the same thing, because he put a hand on her shoulder and whispered something into her ear.

She brushed his hand away, but she walked forward until we were within an arm's reach of each other.

"Pa probably told you," I said. "My mother wanted to be here, but he wouldn't let her. He thought it would bother you too much. She sent you some sandwiches and cookies for the trip. We tried telling her you'd be stopping on the way for dinner, but you know Ma." I shoved the package at her. She took it without saying a word.

This was ever so much harder than telling Pa about Jesse and Mr. Phelps. There was too much to say and too little time. "I know you must hate me," I said, trying to fill in the silence.

"I don't hate you, Charlotte," she said.

"I'm so sorry. About everything. Most especially about Max, though. I'm sorry he died. I want you to know that I understand about Max and how much you loved him. And I want to tell you that Sheriff Graham returned his body to us. We buried him for you. He's under the lilacs, with his mother and his brothers. We even planted bee balm over his grave. For remembrance."

She turned her head, and her voice was tiny when she finally spoke. "Thank you. I'll always remember your kindness."

And your betrayal. The unsaid words hung between us.

"Daniel had to clean Jake's stall and feed chickens. Otherwise he'd have been here."

"No he wouldn't," Jesse said.

I started to protest, but she stopped me. "I don't hate you for telling, Charlie. And I don't hate Daniel for not seeing me off. He will never understand, even loving animals the way he does. And you, Charlie, you'll never understand either, but you're here. I want you to know I appreciate that."

The train's whistle sounded from around the bend just as the First Methodist's chimes struck nine.

"I have to be going now. Tell your mother thank you for the food. Tell her . . . tell her she's a fine lady."

"I haven't told her—or Daniel—about the others. I mean, about what you said the other day. I would never say a word about that."

"Thank you."

"Mrs. Graham came to see Ma. She said she was sorry, that Aaron Phelps was an evil man who should have been stopped a long time ago. Jesse, she meant a whole lot more than that."

"I don't want to know, Charlie. She tried to talk to me herself, but I didn't want to hear it. I still don't. It doesn't make any difference."

It did, at least to me, but I let the subject drop. "I'll write to you."

"Please don't, Charlie," she said. We stood in silence. I shuffled my feet. Jesse held the package in one hand and pleated the folds of her skirt with the other. After the longest time, she spoke again. "You'll always be my best friend, you know. In spite of everything. You were never like Sara Avery and her kind, picking at me because they thought I was an orphan. You liked me, and it never mattered to you where I came from or what awful things I'd done. And that's how best friends are." Her eyes might have misted up some, but Jesse didn't cry. She turned away just then and squared her shoulders. Walking just like she had a yardstick in her back, she marched to where Pa and Sheriff Graham stood waiting for the train to stop. A couple of passengers alighted. As soon as they did, Jesse climbed onto the train without even waiting for Sheriff Graham or the conductor to help her. She disappeared into the car and never once looked back.

My father walked over and placed his arm around my shoulder. "It's time to go home, Sissy."

We watched the train pull out and then walked the length of the station. In the shadows of the building, where Jesse stood when she first arrived in Turner's Crossing, Daniel waited. He didn't say a word when we passed by but fell into step with us as we trudged towards home. When we got there, Pa said, "Sissy, you go tell your mother we're here, and that I'll be going in late to the office. Daniel and I have some clearing out to do in the barn."

Ma was waiting on the back stoop.

"Pa and Daniel are in the barn," I told her.

Ma didn't ask me how I was. She didn't ruffle my hair or straighten my collar. Instead she said, "I admire you so much, Charlotte Anne Matthews."

My face must have registered my shock. "I don't understand."

"I admired your brain when you got all those awards at graduation. I admired your courage when you told your Pa and me about Mr. Phelps. But this mornin', when you went off to say good-bye to Jesse? It must have been awfully hard to go to that train station, not knowin' how you'd be received. I have to tell you, Sissy, I admire the goodness in your heart, and that's most important of all."

"She doesn't hate me, Ma. But she doesn't want me to write."

"Honey, sometimes memories are just too painful."

"Daniel was there at the station, too."

"I know."

"But he didn't say anything to her. He just watched the train leave."

"I know that too, Sissy. You can't blame him for that. He's a good boy, and he'll be a good man one day, but he's hurting too much right now. You can't blame him."

"Jesse didn't cry at all."

"That's because she's bleeding inside. Like Daniel is."

I sat down next to her on the stoop. Suddenly the tears came. She gathered me into her arms and rocked me gently against her body.

"I hate Jesse's father," I told her through my tears.

Ma just squeezed me harder. She didn't understand.

But I didn't always understand her, either. You don't have to understand people to love them. Ma was the one holding me and smoothing my hair and telling me everything would be fine. She was right, too. I had Ma and Pa and Daniel watching out for me. And that's what Jesse had been missing her whole life.

"Jesse told me not to, but someday I'm going to write her a letter. So she'll know we still care what happens to her."

"That's right nice of you, Sissy," Ma said. She brushed the hair back off my forehead.

Maybe in an hour, maybe tomorrow, Ma's fussing with my hair would bother me again. But just for now, I rested my head against her shoulder and closed my eyes.

Epilogue: 1915

Later that summer, I sent Jesse a letter. She never wrote back. After that, I sent one letter each year she was in Chillicothe. She didn't answer any of those, either, and finally the reform school sent one back marked No Forwarding Address. So I stopped writing.

I still think about her, especially when Daniel calls me on the telephone. He sits in his law office up in Harrison County, elbows most likely resting on his desk. I sit in my kitchen in Gilman, Kansas, twisting strands of hair around my finger while we talk maybe about politics or the conflict in Europe. We don't spend much time reminiscing.

Not once in ten years has Daniel mentioned Jesse's name to me. But Ma wrote that whenever he comes home for a visit, he finds some excuse to wander out to the lilac bush behind the house. He sits there for a long time before he begins pulling weeds from the bee balm underneath. Ma watches him from the kitchen window. "Daniel has his own way of remembering," she writes.

I also think about Jesse on summer evenings when the Kansas heat hangs in the air and I have to escape to our front porch to let whatever breeze there is blow across my legs. My little daughter Caroline totters through the yard, swaying this way and that on unsteady legs. She greets everything and everybody with outstretched arms. At two years old, Caroline already has an ease with people I've never had. She's more like Ma than me, with the same determined chin and those fearless eyes.

I expect I won't understand Caroline any better than Ma understood me. But then, understanding isn't as important to me as it once was. Mostly I want to protect Caroline—maybe too much—from a world that isn't entirely gentle. Even now, she doesn't take kindly to my protection. She pulls away from my grasp. "No helping, Mama," she scolds.

Jesse sure would have admired her courage.